Life Without

Life Without

Ken Klonsky

To Sondra who lives her life with love

QUATTRO BOOKS

The publication of *Life Without* has been generously supported by the Canada Council for the Arts and the Ontario Arts Council.

Cover design: Diane Mascherin
Cover image: Luciano Iacobelli
Author's photo: Margaret McPhee
Typography: Grey Wolf Typography
Editor: Luciano Iacobelli

Library and Archives Canada Cataloguing in Publication

Klonsky, Kenneth
    Life without / Ken Klonsky.

Issued also in electronic format.
ISBN 978-1-926802-86-2

    I. Title.

PS8571.L66L54 2012   C813'.54   C2012-900343-3

Published by Quattro Books Inc.
89 Pinewood Avenue
Toronto, Ontario, M6C 2V2
www.quattrobooks.ca

Printed in Canada

To David McCallum, Atif Rafay and Gary Dolin.
Together we've seen the awful truth.

TURANDOT

In the gloomy night an iridescent phantom flies.
It spreads its wings and rises over infinite, black humanity!
Everyone invokes it; everyone implores it!
But the phantom disappears at dawn to be reborn in the heart!
And every night it's born and every day it dies!

CALAF

Yes! It's reborn! It's reborn and, exulting,
It carries me with it, Turandot; it is Hope!

I SLOG ALONG ON the low pile carpet of an empty, brightly lit hotel corridor. I am moving in what I think to be a forward direction, but pass no doors and make no visible progress. An uneasy feeling pervades my soul—what it must feel like in Purgatory—and also something deeper, something inside my chest threatening to detonate like a bomb. Out of nowhere, to my right, a musty smelling man wearing a cheap dark blue suit with a heavy snow of dandruff on the shoulders is walking alongside me. He must be a lawyer, of course he's a lawyer, and, judging from the wear and tear of his discounted suit, he must be a poor lawyer. Everything about him, thinning hair, pasty face, is worn, as if he and his suit together have been dry-cleaned too many times. With this lawyer now at my side, we appear to be making progress. He stops at room 412 and looks back at me, squinting through smudged and cracked glasses. He knocks. Once. Twice. The door opens. We are face to face with a teenager with purple dyed hair, her fulsome body packed tightly into faded blue jeans, a t-shirt above her midriff. Her face is familiar, but her nose and forehead are distorted with hostility. Before my lawyer can get his foot in the door, it slams shut. I hear the deadbolt lock and the chain slide into place. My lawyer, the faded man who doesn't know that death has taken hold of him too, knocks again like a persistent salesman, only this time more forcibly. From inside, a fist or heavy object slams into the door. My supposed lawyer stares back at me, waiting for me to tell him what to do. Isn't he supposed to be leading me? I shrug. He starts out again and I follow. He walks past room 414 and stops at 416. My lawyer—I now wonder what he charges per hour—has a key card for this lock. He slides it into the slot and pulls it out. A small whining sound accompanies a green light. The door opens and we walk into the room. I can see a half-emptied open suitcase on the floor. Some of the clothes from the suitcase have been thrown onto the bed. They are men's clothes, extra-large black dress shirts, slacks, and two striped ties carelessly askew, crossing each other like poisonous snakes. Through the bathroom door, I hear a man showering, singing a familiar song, a Verdi song, *la donna è mobile*, about fickle women. He tries the high C at the end and crashes short of the runway. My faded lawyer has gone further into the room and found something on the other side of the bedspread. He appears to be unaware that a man is showering in the bathroom and may soon be finished. My lawyer smiles at me, holding out a lump of what appears to be gold, a gold nugget. I am uncertain from this distance if it really is a gold nugget or fool's gold. The shower stops. I hear a fan. I stare at the bathroom door with a growing dread. The bathroom door opens; a cloud of steam emerges, then a massive, dripping stomach followed by the rest of the man rubbing his scalp with a towel. I'm afraid he's going to look back and see me. Instead, he turns into the room.

I fear for my lawyer. Has he ducked under the bed? The fat man pulls the bedspread off the bed and twirls it over his head. Clothing flies in every direction. I think the fat man is searching for the nugget. I turn around to open the door, stopping, afraid to make a noise, yet I somehow find myself back out in the hallway unescorted.

I search for my missing lawyer, continuing in the same direction along the corridor. In front of two doors sit room service trays with coffee cups, dishes and metal covers. Honeymooners. *Please do not disturb* signs block the slots. I reach the end of the corridor, happy to know that there is an end. I look out a dusty water-stained window into the parking lot. The sun shines mercilessly on the parked cars. I turn back and knock on door number 488. It opens immediately. My lawyer has been awaiting me; he makes a slight bow with a sweeping gesture of his right arm. The room looks as if a party or a meeting has taken place. Empty liquor bottles are arrayed on the floor. Ashtrays.

"Been here, done that," he says. "Too bad, too bad, been here, done that." Isn't that wrong? Isn't it 'Been there, done that'?

Suddenly my chest explodes. I've lost something vital. No, I've lost someone. Not something. Someone. I know that. I am gasping for air. I am sobbing.

"What the hell! Hey, shut the fuck up!"

"Shut up, Ascher!"

"Hernandez, will you shut him up!"

I touch my face and eyes. No tears. I slide out of the lower bunk bed and bump my right shin on the toilet. A mouse, or judging by the length of its tail, a rat, scurries across my foot.

"Sorry, guys. I'm all right."

"Who gives a shit?"

" 'Sorry, guys.' Are you a faggot or something?"

"Who cares if you're all right? Just as long as you shut up!"

"He cries like a woman."

"He talks like a woman."

"I wish the motherfucker was a woman."

"Get the fuck out. That Ascher dude is my meal ticket."

"You know what I'd do to him if he was a woman?"

"What? What would you do?"

"I'd fuck him so bad, my dick would go up his throat."

"Your what? You ain't got none."

"It grows, man. It grows."

"Man, from what I've seen, Dick Johnson ain't nothing but a midget."

"Keep lookin' at it and you'll see what you get."

"What you gonna do, baby?"

From the top bunk, Hernandez snorts and awakens. He has sleep apnea, maybe a touch of pneumonia, definitely a touch of psychosis. He joins the fray while I take a piss.

"Fucking scumbags! You wake me up!"

"Gonna do something about it, Hernandez?"

"You know what I'm gonna do? You know what I'm gonna do?"

"What are you gonna do? What are you gonna do?"

"I'm gonna cut off your *cojones* and shove them in your mouth." A coughing fit ensues. I cover my face with my free hand.

O

Legal visits take place in the cafeteria. The chairs are made of hard material that looks like plastic but feels like lead. I saw an inmate get hit over the head with one of those things. You could actually hear the skull crack. During meals, while I eat the drab, overcooked slop, I keep my neck on a swivel. During the legal visits, except for the lawyer, the client and a soon-to-be-pensioned guard who sits reading porn at an elevated table at the front, the cafeteria is empty and the linoleum floor, as a result of my handiwork, mopped clean and waxed to a shine.

Fiedler, my lawyer, has a face like a rat. He's a small man with close-cropped hair, protruding ears, a narrow pointed nose, eyes hidden inside their sockets, and two prominent front teeth. He even twitches like a rat. I hear his high-pitched voice talking as if he's repeating himself. "Ascher, you like me to get you something from the machines?"

"Sure, thanks, Fiedler."

"It's okay."

He walks over to the change machine and slides in a bill. He's really a considerate sort, but he does look like a rat, a good rat, like the rat in the French cartoon. Unfortunate to look like that—like having a bad name, Clarence or Wilbur—but you can change your name a lot easier than your looks.

Fiedler now walks over to the food and drink machines with his handful of change like a man in an arcade. The warden wants us to believe that these machines are put there for our enjoyment, a special treat for adult infants who behave themselves, but the grapevine says that the warden is getting her cut. It didn't take long to find out why prisoners are allowed to have large sums of money on deposit. The money is swallowed by the food and the drink machines during visits or sunk into enterprises run from outside the prison by people who left the system to get rich. The prison brass often reminds us to use the mail order catalogues they distribute. Anyone behind bars with access to money is into mail orders: edible food, clothing, watches, jewelry, radios, small TVs, just about anything besides weapons and illegal drugs. Illegal drugs fall into the domain of small business. If the corporations bribe a superintendent, they get exclusive access to a captive audience and charge prices comparable to Macy's. The crows are picking over carrion, us, the living dead.

"Fish, chicken and cheese, or ham and cheese?" Fiedler calls out this question from over at the machines. "The fish at least may be kosher."

"I'll take the chicken."

"Chicken and cheese. Chicken and cheese." Fiedler slides several coins into the slot, then presses a button and reaches into one of the doors for the sandwich. He then puts the sandwich into a microwave, programs it, and steps back.

"What to drink?"

"Diet Pepsi," I yell over. Fiedler slides coins into the drink machine, presses a button and the Pepsi rumbles down a funnel into a receiving bay. A receiving bay, is that the right phrase? I can't remember things with any precision; prison makes me stupid. He collects the sandwich and comes back to the table. I rip open the hot cellophane, take out the soggy sandwich and bite into the roll, scalding my lips and tongue.

"You like that?"

I down half the Pepsi, letting the cold liquid soak my tongue and lips.

"This stuff here? This stuff is filet mignon. Thanks, Fiedler."

"Don't mention it." He sits back and smiles.

"So what brings you here?"

"We finally have a witness who says you were with him *the day of*."

"No shit!"

"Yes. He remembers meeting you on the subway."

"Really?"

"His name is McHenry. You remember McHenry?"

McHenry? A man named McHenry met me on the subway? Maybe. Is this the break in the case that I've been waiting for? "McHenry, McHenry what?"

"John. John McHenry."

John McHenry. The name reminds me of a black folk hero, the steel driving man. "To tell you the truth, Fiedler, I don't remember any John McHenry."

"Maybe I got the name wrong."

What a lawyer! Fiedler swipes a roach off his briefcase, reaches inside and takes out a legal pad. He starts flipping through the pages.

"Here. MacSweeney. Robert MacSweeney."

"How are you going to get me out of here, Fiedler, if you can't even get witnesses' names right?" Fiedler looks hurt. I have to cut the old guy some slack. "Sorry."

"Let's see. MacSweeney says you were with him on the subway the afternoon of the 14th of June, 2009. He was on his way to a ballgame. You talked about baseball."

Damn it, I'm trying, but I don't remember this at all. "Fiedler, where did you find this guy?"

"He called me. He said he read about your case, about how you lost your appeal."

"Where was he during the trial? Do you think he's just a bullshit artist?"

"Even if he is—so what? That's the day it happened!"

"I know that. Don't you think I know that? Not a day goes by that I don't think about that day. MacSweeney might be making it up. People these days will do anything for publicity."

"You got to look at the bright side. It's what he's prepared to say to a judge. Don't forget, Joel, you lost your appeal."

"We lost."

"Have it your way. We need new evidence if we're going to be able to reopen the case."

"MacSweeney is not exactly DNA."

"MacSweeney *is* new evidence."

"If MacSweeney gets caught in a lie, it'll bury me for good."

"Look, he said you met him on the Lexington Avenue Subway, the number 6 train, right? Sunday noon. The train got stuck for a long time. You talked to him about baseball. Then after the subway started up again, you got off at Union Square and he stayed on for Yankee Stadium. A slice of cake." Fiedler lightly claps his hands.

"I don't remember meeting anyone. Besides, I had to walk through the subway tunnel that day. Don't you remember?"

"Okay, okay, so I didn't get the details straight. He walked through the tunnel with you and he took the express from Union Station."

"The uptown trains stopped running, Fiedler."

"Right. Right. But he stayed down there and waited until they started back up. What's the difference? What's important is that witnesses lied to put you in prison. Even if MacSweeney is lying—but he's not."

A thought occurs to me, a bad thought. "Are you paying this guy?"

Fiedler smiles. "It's not legal to pay witnesses, Joel. Not to say that getting you out of here wouldn't do wonders for my reputation."

Fiedler looks inside his briefcase again. He probes gently and keeps looking up at me, his lower lip twitching below the protruding incisors. I'm thinking he'll take out a piece of cheese and a knife. He pulls out a piece of paper instead.

"An affidavit. See."

Sure enough, Robert MacSweeney, date of birth, February 4th, 1962, signed an affidavit stating that on his way to a Yankee game on June 14th, 2008, he met me on the subway. Good except for one problem.

"Fiedler, it was 2009! You have to change this!"

"Yeah, you're right. I'll prepare a new affidavit and get him to sign again."

Could it be? "Did you check if they were playing that day? Who they were playing?"

"Good suggestions, Joel."

"I really don't think this will fly, Fiedler. Don't you think Glenda is more promising?"

Fiedler stares blankly.

"The one who said she saw me leave the apartment around one o'clock!"

"Glenda?"

"You forgot? Glenda, the liar? Did you try to speak to her about a recantation?"

"Oh, that one. She's stubborn."

"Stubborn? What kind of lawyer are you? You have to deal with stubborn people all the time."

"I'm no Johnnie Cochran, may he rest in peace."

"That's who I need. Johnnie Cochran. 'If the glove don't fit...' How does that go?"

"Johnnie Cochran? He's dead."

"'If the glove don't fit...'"

"The gloves. The gloves."

"'If the gloves don't fit'—what the hell was it?"

"'You must acquit'. Cochran is dead, I tell you!"

"'If the gloves don't fit, you must acquit'. Now that was a lawyer!" If Johnnie Cochran could get O.J. out of that box, he could easily have saved me.

Fiedler is saying something. "Don't 'misunderestimate' me. 'Misunderestimate'. That's Bush. The moron Bush. Now that was a president!"

Fiedler is making jokes while I'm stuck sharing a prison cell with a guy who has paranoid delusions and who snores like a calliope. Calliope! I live three feet from a rancid toilet bowl. The stink, the rats, the roaches, the noise, the shouting, the garbage music never stops. I haven't slept in three years.

"Fiedler, you have *got* to get me out of here!"

"You can't rush the law, Joel. The law takes her sweet time. You got plenty of books I bought you. You said you like mysteries; I bought you mysteries. You said you like poetry; I bought you poetry, the biggest poetry book in the whole store."

"But they're all by the same poet. Did you know you bought me 1775 poems by Emily Dickinson?"

"She's good, no?"

"I need some variety."

"Take a course already. Don't they offer poetry courses? You're a smart man. A smart man needs intellectual distraction. Otherwise, it's hard to be patient."

"Come switch places with me and see how patient you'd be."

"You might have given that a little thought before you confessed."

His comment slices into me, a knife between my ribs. "I didn't know what I was saying! I was so tired." Why do I need to explain to this man what he already knows?

"Do you know how hard it is to overturn a confession? After you been read your Mirandas?"

"Anyone would have broken down! Anyone!"

"I guess so, under the circumstances maybe."

"You're goddamned right under the circumstances! And where were you that day while my ass was getting fried? In fucking Yonkers!"

"Okay. Okay. Cool off. I'm doing what I can. Let me add MacSweeney to your 440 motion."

"MacSweeney."

"You might want to meet him first before you make judgments."

"I'm not making judgments."

Fiedler checks his watch. It's a Timex, a diving watch.

"Do you snorkel?" I ask him, trying to imagine this skinny old guy in a bathing suit somewhere in the warm blue Hawaiian sea. As he starts putting the documents back into the briefcase, he looks up at me.

"Why do you ask?"

"Never mind."

"No, what's this with snorkeling?"

"It doesn't matter."

He looks at me with concern. "I'll bring MacSweeney next time."

"When will that be?"

"Soon."

Despite myself, he's hooked me again. Maybe I did meet some guy named MacSweeney? Maybe he was the guy who came on to the subway right behind me? The blue and white stained polo shirt. I couldn't figure out what that stain was on his protruding belly. Kool-Aid? Beets? Blood? Was he wearing a Yankees cap? Did I speak to him? Maybe. Maybe I have amnesia?

As Fiedler stands up, Williams, a wiry young guard with wire-rimmed glasses who has been standing by the door leading back to the prison, comes over. With a big smile on his light brown face, he rips open a package of latex gloves. I stand too. Fiedler reaches out his hand to me and I shake it. Then he draws me into a hug.

"I'm going to get you out of here, Joel. Don't misunderestimate me."

"I won't, Fiedler."

Fiedler, the back of his blue suit shiny and crumpled, heads for the exit to the free world. That's what we call it, where humanity lives: the free world.

"Let's go, *Mister* Ascher, if it pleases your royal majesty." Williams, with a slight bow and an arm extended, is motioning for me to follow. We stop outside an opaque glass booth where a guard inside presses a button and a heavy gray steel door next to the booth slides slowly open. We walk inside a room that looks like a subterranean vault. The door slides closed behind us. Williams and I are now encased inside a no man's land of painted steel and bulletproof glass, state of the art prison technology, physically and psychologically inescapable. America, I think with pride, the source of most of the world's great inventions, engineering marvels, bridges, skyscrapers, the Metropolitan Opera, home to creativity and innovation, is without question the world's leading expert in prisons. America had a lot of practice rounding up Indians and slaves, throwing them into stockades and destroying their psyches until her prisons reached their current state of perfection.

Smiling in my face, Williams snaps a glove on his left wrist and then one on the right. He wrinkles up his nose.

"Something stinks in here, my man. Bad. Whew!"

The steel door in front of us slides open and we walk out. We stop in sight of another opaque glass window where another guard is sitting, no doubt whacking off.

"Open your mouth, Ascher man." Williams takes out a pen-sized flashlight, places his right index finger on my tongue and shines the light inside. "Good. No capsules, no plastic bags. But you might try flossing, man."

"Get me some floss. Please. I'd kill for floss. My nails are broken."

"That can be arranged but it'll cost. Anything else you need, my brother?"

"No. Not from you anyway. Wait, come to think of it, how about a fungicide?"

"For what?"

"For a fungus! What else? Inside my navel. That's what stinks."

Williams lifts my shirt and pokes my spare tire with the flashlight. "You got an innie. Them funguses love innies. It's dark and damp down there. You need to get your ass in shape, Ascher. Get out in the yard. Run. Pump the weights, man. Open that thing up to the air."

The last thing I need now is a pep talk.

"You want fungicide? Over the counter shit is cheap but it don't work half the time. Prescription, that's what I recommend. Prescription. But that'll cost."

"Prick," I mutter.

"Talk nice, offender Ascher. Number 09B-3448. Remember where you are, my man. The Department of Corrections don't like it when you verbally abuse the guards."

"When can you get it?" I see another guard coming down the hallway, Sergeant Kelton, a beefy mustachioed guy I wouldn't want to meet in an alley, dark or light. Williams sees him too.

"Okay, spread 'em, Ascher," Williams says, while his superior, chewing on his handlebar mustache, looks on.

I pull down my pants. While I bend over, Williams opens my anus with his thumb and forefinger, shining the light up there. "You're clean, offender Ascher."

I glare at him.

"You don't like that, my man? Would you rather I did your mouth second?"

"What's the point of this routine? It's degrading."

Kelton stares at me as if I've just said the most absurd thing in the world.

"You think my lawyer is going to bring in drugs?"

"You don't like the regs, offender Ascher?" Kelton booms. "We can always send you up to Attica." He goes on his way. To where, I don't know. Guards are always walking from one place to another. They walk; they push buttons to slide doors open; they check anuses; they make smart remarks to prisoners. Sometimes they break up fights and sometimes they beat up an inmate. Maybe their most important job is counting us three times each day, as they do kindergarten children on a field trip.

The prisoners do the work of the prison. They cook; they clean; they do laundry; they run the library; they dig the graves. Some work in small industry. We have a unit of felons that, for twenty-eight cents an hour, double the usual rate, makes army helmets. Even the military needs to cut back on expenses.

When Kelton disappears, Williams drops his wise guy attitude, speaking softly now. "Believe me, I don't got it any better than you. Look at the shit I gotta do."

"You can go home at night, Williams."

"It's not so good there, I can tell you, man."

"Just give me one night at home."

"Yeah? You got children?"

"No, I don't."

"Children. Now that's a prison."

"If you don't mind my saying this, Williams, that's not smart."

"Maybe not."

"I used to think a child would mess up my life. You should know how lucky you are. Go home and hug your kid and tell him how much you love him."

"Boy and a girl, man."

"And while you're at it, hug your wife."

Williams goes silent. Something I said has registered—for both of us. He stares at me.

"What's that fungicide you were talking about, Williams?"

"Lamisil's the best."

"Lamisil. When did you become a fucking pharmacist?"

"Live and learn, man. Live and learn. You don't even have to do no degree. Lamisil and tea tree oil. Works on the feet too—if you got leftovers. Look, I do you a favor, my man, because I like you. You buy the Lamisil and the tea tree oil; I throw in the floss."

"Why don't you throw in the tea tree oil too?"

"Stuff's organic, man. Stuff costs."

"All right. What's it gonna run me?"

"Eighty. Minimum."

"Jesus. You mind telling me how much you're getting on the deal?"

"This ain't no business, my man. You think I'm runnin' some business? It's a service. You run a service, you take risks. You gotta cover my risk."

The loudspeaker sounds. "Count!"

"Okay," I nod to Williams. "Lamisil and whatever else you said." I walk off.

O

Back in the hotel hallway with my faded lawyer, I'm feeling compelled to brush off the shoulders of his suit; I'd do it if only I could. He runs a hand through his thinning red hair, producing more snow. We are now going up the side of the hallway with odd numbers. He stops at 437, looks back at me. This time he uses the side of his fist. Blam! Blam! Blam! The door opens. It's a female nurse wearing a white uniform, white running shoes, a shower cap on her head and a surgical mask on her face. Inside the room is an operating table beneath a white-hot operating lamp. A surgeon, also masked, and from her shape I can see she's also a woman, is standing at the ready holding a shiny implement. My lawyer gently takes my left arm, the nurse the right. They help me remove my shoes and clothes. They escort me to the table where I lie down. As I lie there, the surgeon, without a calming word, cuts into the skin alongside my stomach, right into my spare tire. I feel no pain. She lifts out a square of innards, molten and red like a piece of lasagna, covered by a layer of epidermis. The nurse replaces the chunk with a plug. Cork? Tobacco? My faded lawyer comes over and helps me up from the table. I'm wobbly. He leads me out the door and back into the hallway. I've forgotten my clothes. I am standing stark naked in the motel hallway. I have to make sure that the plug is firmly in place. It's not. There's seepage. My lawyer looks on with alarm. I bang on the door.

O

Being on trial for a crime I did not commit was, I thought, not dissimilar from Jesus nailed to the crucifix, hanging above the rabble while they gawked at him obscenely. In a courtroom, people stare at a defendant from two directions, the jury from in front and the spectators from behind. Some spectators were there to watch my crucifixion, my agony being their entertainment, and some to see a morality play. The jury, predisposed, as in all cases, to believing the prosecutor, looked at me for character flaws or inappropriate behavior. My school report cards were full of *inappropriate behaviors*, as in *Joel demonstrates inappropriate behaviors*. How would someone like me fare under the pressure of all those eyes? If I was going to stand a chance, Fiedler told me, they had to identify with me; they had to see me in the same way that they saw themselves.

Fiedler crossed swords with a young, red-faced, Type A alpha-male prosecutor named Brookes, who usually wore a black pinstriped suit and had a disconcerting habit of running his hand through a heavily greased-back head of hair. Actually, they didn't cross swords. Alpha/Brookes had a sword; Fiedler had a butter knife. Fiedler had never won an acquittal going up against this vain, ambitious prick, but my lawyer is a man of unflagging hope, the kind who gets thrown into the dirt time after time but, unlike me, keeps coming back at his tormentor. You have to love him for his, his, his what? His indefatigability.

Eventually, six men and six women of varying ages wound up on the panel. Three of the women were professionals: a middle-aged business executive with square tortoise shell eyeglasses, who wore pantsuits made of shiny material; an

African American copy editor from a women's magazine who filed her nails with an emery board; and an elementary teacher who seemed relieved to be away from a roomful of rambunctious brats. During selection, Alpha/Brookes showed considerable skill.

To the three professionals, partially hidden amongst a series of innocuous questions, he asked, "How do you balance family and professional career?" He wanted to see if they might identify with Marsha as a mother-to-be and an aspiring lawyer. Fiedler, on the other hand, only asked if they could look at evidence objectively.

"Fiedler," I whispered, "those three will hang me."

"They're educated. They'll see you as educated. Education counts for a lot."

"Marsha was the one who was educated. I'm a cab driver."

"Shhh." What did I have to do with it anyway? The process of selection took two sessions. Two sessions to choose a jury for a big murder trial! A stern looking grandmother, who was chosen forelady, forewoman, foreperson, whatever, was the fourth juror. I was convinced that number five, a middle-aged medical secretary with dyed blond hair, was more of a spectator than a juror, an audience member of a reality TV show. Four senior males, all in varying stages of gray, white, silver or disappeared hair, two who thought the fetus was a person and the other two who took a dim view of adultery, also made it on to the panel. Fiedler let me know that this was a trade off. It made me sick to think that Fiedler might have no faith in my case and was already preparing a fallback defense, aggravated homicide in the face of adultery. The two anti-abortionists spent the trial staring dolefully at me like bishops at the Inquisition. One of the others, bald on top, whose remaining hair stuck out as if his finger was caught in a socket, could fall asleep with his eyes open. Fiedler thought he was a former hippie but never explained to me why that would help. The fourth senior male, chosen ninth, a seemingly wise Japanese man with silver hair and a narrow silver beard that hung down like the tail of a kite, smiled at me for most of the trial. Fiedler said that smiling was a good sign for the defendant. The tenth member chosen for the panel was a real triumph for Fiedler, or so he thought: a massive bald guy with a tattoo on his neck who looked as if he should have been wearing a studded leather jacket. Instead, he was stuffed uncomfortably into a sport jacket that was ready to burst at the armpits. Fielder figured that this guy wouldn't even see wife killing as a crime. "Just in case things start going southerly, you got one vote here that will hang the whole shebang."

Trouble was that he missed the significance of a key question from Alpha/Brookes. When the prosecutor asked Mr. Hell's Angel if he believed in retribution, the giant said, "Shit yes." Fiedler thought that he was referring to the lawless code of the gang. Alpha/Brookes tried to repress a smile; he knew that he'd found a Christian, a born again motorcycle Christian. Disaster. Turns out he led the charge against me. A guy on a jury who says *shit* yes!

The other two were blue-collar workers, a Sikh postman with a deviated septum whose breathing annoyed his fellow jurors, and a female air conditioning repairwoman who had been laid off and seethed with bitterness. I told Fiedler that most of these people would take a dim view of a wife killer.

He laughed. "Joel, don't forget that you're an innocent man."

How right he was. What was I saying?

"What we need on the panel are people who can believe in your innocence. These people I chose have open minds. I've given you a fighting chance."

During my trial, when I turned briefly to face the crowd, I could see that the courtroom spectators were almost all from Marsha's wide circle of family and friends, some of whom I had seen at our wedding. When I turned back to face the judge, their malignant stares burned a hole in my neck. They heard

Fiedler, wearing a distracting herringbone sport jacket; the young slickly dressed and greased down prosecutor; the black robed judge, Judge Poliakoff, a very small and surprisingly young looking woman with cherry red lipstick and dyed jet black hair puffed into a Jackie Kennedy bouffant; and an array of witnesses all talking about me. The more the jury and the people in the courtroom heard the case being tried, the less they identified with me.

That was me the court officers were talking about, but no one talked to me. Despite Fiedler's efforts, everything they said confirmed that I was an outlaw. The judge, the jury, the whole courtroom, this whole damn city full of people, if their lives could be revealed, enough shit could be found there to prosecute. Scratch the surface and you would find abusers, assaulters, embezzlers, tax evaders, thieves, and rapists, even murderers. But since the people in that courtroom were not into looking at themselves—doing a 'There but for the grace of God'—and since they came to believe that I killed Marsha, the shoes had to be made to fit me, the killer. Fiedler was wrong. They were not open-minded. Or they may have been until Alpha/Brookes tapped into their latent fury about what they thought I had done, by showing crime scene photos at strategic moments.

The case against me consisted of my so-called confession, an argument in a parking lot, a girl who thought she saw me leave the apartment when I was really stuck down in a subway, a police officer's testimony, a minor spat in a restaurant, a violation of doctor/patient confidentiality, an unethical forensic psychiatrist, and Marsha's blood on my right hand and the right side of my clothing.

A young Latino couple saw me argue with Marsha in the parking lot of a Home Depot in Queens. They said I humiliated her. What were we arguing about in that parking lot? Shelving. Don't all couples argue about shelving?

"C'mon, Marsha, let's just decide. We can go back in and get the metal shelves if you want or we can go back to IKEA for the melamine." I felt sure she wouldn't want to schlep back to Long Island.

"I don't think it's called 'Ikeeya', Joel. It's 'Ikaya'.

"You're wrong but who the fuck cares?"

"Joel, you're getting distraught again. I tell you what: let's go look at some real wooden shelves. I like real wood better than the ersatz stuff. I love blond wood; it's just like a baby's hair. There's a funky furniture store on 72nd Street."

"Jesus Christ! It's a waste of money. Wooden shelves, blond wooden shelves, in a baby's room!"

Marsha broke down in tears. She said I was being an asshole, but I think she was being labile, which is common during pregnancy. Whatever the case, I feel like hell when I cause someone to cry. In the end, we got the blond shelves. They cost enough to get me an airline flight to Australia, not that I'll be going there any time soon. I never saw the Latino couple in the parking lot, but they came forward when the case hit the media. Two straightforward and honest people, they were convincing witnesses. Fiedler's cross-examination consisted of asking them if they were certain that it was me they saw in the parking lot. They were.

Glenda Romanowski, a teenager with attitude, insisted on having seen me come out of my building between one and one-thirty on the day of the murder. If the jury believed that, my alibi was blown. Alpha/Brookes constructed a theory that I had killed Marsha after one o'clock, left the building, and come back an hour or so later, pretending to discover her body with the blood beginning to coagulate.

"Or maybe," he allowed, "the defendant, like my learned colleague told you, did go down earlier to buy a record, have a coffee and read *The Times*, but he was back inside the apartment by one o'clock. That's when he killed Marsha. The key point is that the witness told you she saw Mr. Ascher coming out the door a short time later."

He said that my alibi was constructed when I found out that the Lexington Avenue subway had been stuck that day. It didn't help that we were unable to produce a single witness who saw me down there.

Glenda said I behaved like a man who had just committed murder. Fiedler raised an objection that her testimony amounted to pointless speculation, swelling with pride when the judge sustained it. Alpha/Brookes, undeterred, got her to describe my crumpled outfit smeared with blood and my harried appearance.

Fiedler tried to establish doubt about Glenda's testimony.

"Isn't it a fact that you act in high school dramas?"

"So?"

"The witness will answer 'yes' or 'no'," ordered the judge.

"Isn't it a fact that you act—"

"Yeah, all right."

"Isn't it a fact," he said, "that your real name is Glinda? Didn't you change your name so that you could have the name of a famous actress?" She stared confusedly at Fiedler but didn't answer. He did get her to admit that she'd seen a news report with me being led out of the building. Fiedler accused her of fantasizing in order to garner publicity for Facebook.

Alpha/Brookes' recross established that Glinda was the good witch in *The Wizard of Oz*, and a bigger star than Glenda Jackson. Truthfully, I couldn't imagine a teenager knowing a thing about Glenda Jackson, but this was a court of law, where common sense has no place whatsoever.

"All right," said Fiedler to Glinda/Glenda, "no one else saw my client in the street with blood on his hands and shirt. How is this possible? The doorman didn't see him in that condition either. How is this possible unless you're fantasizing?"

"Objection!"

"I'll withdraw the question."

A further debate about Glenda/Glinda and the kinds of things that people might or might not perceive on a very hot day went on. The medical secretary began to stretch and pop the gum she was chewing. Judge Poliakoff didn't seem to hear it. The copy editor put down her emery board and opened up a jar of skin cream. Scooping out the cream with her index finger, she rubbed her hands slowly and elegantly together. The key lime smell pervaded the courtroom. By the time Glenda stepped down from the witness stand, I thought that Fiedler had at least gotten a draw.

The subway alibi took a significant hit when a rare record store proprietor from Greenwich Village was called to the stand. "*Oy vey*," said Fiedler, knowing well, since he had gone to the store himself, that this gentleman had no recollection of me being there *the day of.*

I told the police that I'd been down there that morning searching for a rare LP, Callas's live version of *La Traviata.* The proprietor, a fussy middle-aged man, an obsessive-compulsive, didn't remember me being there that day even though I walked right past him at the counter. I prefer to do my own searching and, since I knew where the Verdi LP's were located, I didn't stop to speak to him.

No one interrupted the proprietor of the record store when he began, at Alpha/Brookes' prompting, to talk about his collection. The secretary continued to snap her gum, the popping noise getting louder, and did so at regular intervals, once every twenty seconds according to the court clock. The businesswoman kept removing her tortoise shell glasses, rubbing the bridge of her nose and putting them back on. The magazine copy editor went back to her emery board while the court still smelled of her skin cream. The guy who slept with his eyes open kept nodding off and snapping his head back into place. The wise and happy old man with the kite tail beard kept smiling at me. After a while I lost faith in Fiedler's assessment; I don't think he was wise at all. The Hell's Angel glowered, never for a moment letting up on me.

"You might want to come down and see my *bel canto* collection," the proprietor said. Alpha/Brookes appeared to have fixed his gaze on some spectator in the courtroom I could not see. "My Bellini is second to none, five separate full length versions of *Norma* alone. My Donizetti contains sixteen separate recordings of Dame Joan. Oh, and my Sills..." The only person the least bit interested in the wares of his store was me.

The sounds coming from the jury became as rhythmical as a morning on Catfish Row. The bishops played a duet, one of them rolling his rosary beads, the other clacking his false teeth like a skeleton. The postal worker's clogged sinuses sounded like a man drowning. The bitter repairwoman cracked her knuckles severely. The copy editor filed away with the emery board. The gum kept popping. The stern grandmother kept looking in vain for the judge to assert some discipline.

Fiedler's eyes glazed over. Alpha/Brookes, looking off into the distance like a sailor with a telescope, seemed unaware that the witness was even talking. The spectators in the courtroom chatted. The proprietor kept on yammering. I began to think that the problem with Judge Poliakoff was her height, or lack of it. All that appeared of her, way up there on the bench, was her face and the bouffant, so she couldn't see what was happening beneath her. Here I was being tried for murder and a courtroom of adults was behaving like twelve-year-old kids whose teacher had stepped out of the classroom. Or maybe all trials had moments like these where everyone took a rest, everyone except that damned Hell's Angel who kept his attention fixed squarely on me. Like all cowards, I've always attracted bullies.

Alpha/Brookes, as if awakening, interrupted the proprietor and asked him if he had ever seen me before.

Looking straight at me, the proprietor said, "I know that man. Of course I know him. He was a regular. Very big on the heavies, Wagner and Verdi."

"And you didn't see him on Sunday, June the fourteenth, 2009, did you?"

"Objection," said Fiedler.

"All right, I'll rephrase it. Did you see him in your store on Sunday, June fourteenth, 2009?" I noticed that the jury was once again paying attention.

"I can say categorically that the defendant was not in my store that morning."

"No more questions."

Fiedler then approached the witness. "Isn't it a fact that your store has many aisles and an area in the rear that are out of your vision?"

"Yes. But everyone goes by me coming in and going out." The proprietor looked at me. "You weren't there and you know it! You haven't bought a record in six months!" So that was it. His business had probably declined and he saw me as a scapegoat. He would never have missed me coming in.

Judge Poliakoff was not happy. "Witness will confine his answers to counsel. You are not to address the defendant!"

Fiedler, to his credit, I suppose, asked nothing more.

The police officer, actually a captain, a man with a very red face, even redder than Alpha/Brookes, and very white hair, red and white like a barbershop pole, told the court what I said about Marsha: "She could be a royal pain in the butt." I remember how serious he looked, writing on his pad, when he heard that. What I really said was that even though she could be a royal pain in the butt, *I loved her to death.* That was a bad expression too in hindsight. You never know what you're going to say in that situation, especially if you tend to say inappropriate things in the first place.

In court, the barber pole captain, Captain Swain, the man who eventually became my interrogator, described what he called my "callous disregard." Never in his twenty-six years on the force had he seen a less emotional man in the face of such a "harrowing tragedy." I never expected to hear a cop speak like a film critic from *The New Yorker.*

In his cross-examination, Fiedler got him to admit that I may have been in shock and didn't know what I was saying.

Then Fiedler said, irrelevantly, I thought, and to no one in particular, that my emotional life had been blunted by cab driving, having to deal with the constant aggravation of the job. All he had done was set me up for a well-timed counter punch.

Alpha/Brookes reminded the jury of my love for opera. "This man usually wears his heart on his sleeve. Except for when he covers up a cold and calculating crime. The crime of murdering the wife he no longer loved."

"Objection," chirped Fiedler.

"Yes?" asked the judge while Fiedler sorted out the objection in his mind.

"The fact that my client likes opera is irrelevant and immaterial and also prejudicial."

Brookes shot back, "I was simply answering my learned colleague's assertion that Mr. Ascher's emotional life had been blunted."

"Whatever," said Judge Poliakoff.

"I want my objection as part of the record," ordered Fiedler.

"Noted."

I had never thought about either side of this argument until it came out in the courtroom. When I did think about it, I was struck by the conviction that Fiedler was right; Alpha/Brookes was hinting to the jury about something underneath the surface of the argument. Something prejudicial, as Fiedler said. Since most people do not love opera—do not even like opera one bit—I was separated as an elitist from the jury. How clever of Alpha/Brookes, encouraging the proprietor to bore the jury and have their hatred of the art form re-enforced. And maybe something even subtler was at play here. This was not about the crime; this was about me, or what he wanted the jury to think about me. My love of opera and my heart on my sleeve were signs that I was a gay, or even, God forbid, closeted. The prosecutor's assertion that Marsha was the wife I no longer loved sounded more credible. It dawned on me then that lawyers are either good or bad storytellers.

The next witness was a young waiter with a shaved head who worked at Ferruci's Trattoria. During lunch, this young waiter stood waiting. Yes, the waiter waited, and not too patiently, for Marsha to order. Did she want the veal chop or the vodka pasta? The bald waiter, bald by choice, tapped my menu in his palm, waiting for Marsha to hand him her menu. This went on for what seemed like ten minutes but was probably less. I was just hungry and tired and thinking that having a baby was going to be a big mistake. And that damned waiter kept tapping the menu like Chinese water torture.

"What about the halibut, Madam? The halibut special?" He had already described the halibut as being encrusted with macadamia nuts and served with garlic mashed potatoes but he did it again. No doubt the guy loved food; he was practically drooling. Marsha was now perplexed; his description of the halibut overwhelmed her. It was as if, in choosing an entrée, he'd asked her to recite the Four Questions at the Seder table.

I couldn't stand it anymore. "Marsha! Just order something!" Then I grabbed away her menu and ordered for her. "Get her the fucking veal chop already!"

"I want the halibut," she said to the waiter who was beginning to look frightened. "Joel, I like to play with possibilities. You know that I like to play with possibilities!" She burst into tears, got up and left the table. Why couldn't she just make up her mind? The waiter with the shaved head smirked at me, "Can I get you a drink, sir?" I asked for a Scotch, not that I did any more than sip it. I never drink Scotch but it seemed like the manly thing to do. A glass of red wine would have seemed too laid back. I was unpleasantly surprised to hear that he would be testifying against me too. In court, he said he was sure that I was capable of murder; that I was simmering with rage, a pot about to boil, and other kitchen metaphors.

I still feel terrible about that incident. I might have tried to understand her, her need to play with possibilities, but I was my angry and impatient self. I failed in every aspect of marriage. If

I wasn't losing my temper, I was preoccupied with useless garbage: where to park my taxicab; how to get through my pile of magazines; what time to play my online poker; when to watch the baseball game. I was a child when it came to women. I was a child, period. When I talked to her, it was only to tell her about me. To this day, I don't know what she thought about most things. As to what she felt, I know even less. I see her in my mind's eye, listening sympathetically, listening and responding. It makes me hate myself even now.

At that point, Alpha/Brookes played the final moment of my confession, my supposed confession, to the courtroom. They first heard Captain Swain:

So you say it was possible that you killed Marsha?

And then they heard my response. *Sure. I told you. And who knows who else I killed?*

By then, the noise in the courtroom had stopped. I could see that the jury was outraged by my supposed flippancy. It was confirmation of my being a sociopath. Even the not-so-wise and happy man was no longer amused. The Hell's Angel's face contorted into a vicious sneer. Were we outside the courtroom, he'd have squeezed me shut and opened me up like an accordion. This was not to be the last time they would hear those lines either.

For me, personally, the most devastating witness was our doctor, our own family doctor, Dr. Pearlstone, who later that week told the court that I was very conflicted about having a child. I was being honest with him and he goes and spills out my private thoughts in a courtroom. Tell me who isn't conflicted about children? To have your life turned into shit, piss, vomit, soccer teams and SUV's. Being forced to move out to the suburbs and be enslaved by the chain stores. Dr. Pearlstone agonized, he said. He agonized—give me a break—over whether to violate confidentiality. He told a hushed courtroom that he felt terribly but he had to do it.

The jury could barely conceal their amusement when my brother, Ed, at Fiedler's behest, said that I was *a devoted husband*. The secretary tittered. They looked at each other knowingly, which they are not supposed to do and which Judge Poliakoff, as usual, failed to see. I wondered if the jury also noticed that my parents weren't there to testify.

My friend, Goldfarb, was the next witness. He said that I had a great sense of humor and was loyal to a fault. As he told some sentimental story about visiting a mutual friend dying of cancer in the hospital and how I made the poor guy laugh, the gum popped. As if on signal, the jurors were back in their own separate worlds again.

Finally, we had to deal with a forensic psychiatrist, a polished speaker who wore a tight black revealing skirt. The prosecutor read out a lengthy list of credentials.

"That little *pisher*, Brookes, told her to dress that way," Fiedler whispered, "It's the oldest trick in the books." As if in confirmation of Fiedler's assessment, the two bishops, the sleeper, the postal worker and the wise man, all the men on the jury except the Hell's Angel, who still kept his gaze fixed on me, perked up, staring at her with such beatific smiles you would have thought that they were seeing a vision of the Holy Virgin, a Holy Virgin wearing a tight black skirt who kept shifting her knees from side to side. She said that men like me sometimes kill pregnant wives because we feel cornered. We are afraid that our selfish lives will be impinged upon. And, yes, it was perfectly consistent that I might have blacked out and committed the crime. Echoing testimony from the barber pole, she said, "One part of him, the law-abiding Joel, didn't want to know what the other part, the outlaw Joel, was doing." She likened me to women who kill their children during bouts of postpartum depression except, for some reason, she said that the outlaw Joel's crime, unlike theirs, was premeditated. What could I have said to Fiedler or the jury: that the murder I didn't commit wasn't premeditated?

"But," asked Fiedler, falling into a trap as usual, "if my client didn't know what he was doing, then he wouldn't be guilty of murder, would he?" The court was hushed again after this blunder. The psychiatrist smirked. My lawyer had essentially said that I'd done the crime. He tried to backtrack. "Not that he killed his wife in any way shape or form, mind you. I was just asking you the question to make a point of philosophy."

"Objection," said Alpha/Brookes quietly. "We're not here to discuss philosophy." Even while doing this, you could see that he was feeling sorry for Fiedler. Not that he felt sorry for me.

"Counsel will keep his questions more focused."

"No more questions, Your Honor." Fiedler sat down dejectedly.

As the trial progressed, Fiedler decided that I should not testify on my own behalf. He could see that I had worked myself into a state of fear about Alpha/Brookes. The sight of him and his greased-down hair made me paranoid. That slick and shiny shock of black hair would slide me straight down to perdition. I wouldn't be able to hold my own against his cross-examination. What if he produced my old school report cards in court? Or dug up some of my former teachers from the grave? He would too. He was that thorough.

Next morning, the summations came and then the charge to the jury. Blind justice was moving along quickly.

Then came the moment when the jury returned and the dowdy forewoman, the stern and loving grandmother, stood up. They'd taken just three hours, a bad sign, as anyone would tell you. Fear took hold of my digestive tract. Fiedler took hold of my hand.

They found me guilty of course. Murder one. Found me guilty of the premeditated murder of my wife and, as mentioned and implied many times by Alpha/Brookes, my baby to be. The whole court let out a little cheer and a concerted sigh of relief. The judge was pleased. No more mystery to be solved, no doubt, no uncertainty. Closure, they call it. Everyone was relieved, everyone except my brother, Ed and my friend, Goldfarb. My brother looked embarrassed; he was embarrassed at having to testify falsely about my relationship with Marsha and at having me for a brother. Goldfarb went over to Marsha's family and friends and hugged them as they wept. I think he was apologizing for what I'd done or maybe what he'd done. They had heard the truth, the whole truth and nothing but the truth, just as the court clerk kept admonishing the witnesses. The jury decided whose truth they believed and the truth they believed, the truth of Alpha/Brookes, was that I was a wife killer. That is what I was, a wife killer, the real truth notwithstanding. I was a wife killer, not even a convicted wife killer. It was yet another victory for young Alpha/Brookes over old Fiedler. And the truth, the whole truth, was that I felt at that moment that they must be right—yet they weren't.

Fiedler, God bless his little rat face, put his arm around my shoulder. "Not to worry. Not to worry. We've got them on appeal. Your Fifth Amendment rights were massacred." I stared at him thinking that he could just go on and ply his trade, knowing that another payday was coming in the appeals court. "And if, God forbid, we lose the appeal, we'll hire a private investigator to find the real murderer." *We'll hire* meant that *I, Ascher, will hire.* Of course, we did lose the appeal a year later; my confession was deemed to be constitutional.

During my sentencing by Judge Poliakoff, I wanted to scream. *Look, you fuckheads! Look at me! Don't you see that I'm innocent? I would never kill anyone! Especially my wife! I loved Marsha! I loved her!* Of course I wouldn't scream that out in court, much for the same reason you don't punch a guard in the mouth. They tell you that another chance is coming, an appeal, the possibility of parole, however remote. Screaming in court would be an inexcusable infraction.

You don't want to commit an infraction of any sort under the jurisdiction of the legal system. In prison, they put you in solitary confinement for major infractions. It's not really a hole anymore but it is deafeningly quiet. What's the difference anyway? I'm already in a hole, this whole prison, and, with the shoddy work of my incompetent rat-faced lawyer, my body will run its natural course. Then another hole—I've seen a graveyard in the shadows behind the prison yard—awaits me. If no relatives show up to reclaim the body, the body, my body that will have expired, is slated for burial in that hole. A chaplain, I think it will be a chaplain, whatever a chaplain is, whatever religion he represents, will say some words over me, some non-denominational hocus pocus, make some solemn gestures, and my coffin will be lowered into this other hole like lading lowered into the belly of a ship. The graveyard is small and so many people have been killed or died of disease in this place, so many people who have been forgotten, that my coffin will hang suspended while prisoners pull out two other coffins, designating one for disposal, before I am lowered to the bottom. But that may not even happen until forty or fifty years from now, those years ahead, those *deserts of vast eternity.*

I didn't scream out in that courtroom. I cried. Involuntarily. I cried for my dead wife, my non-existent child and for the life that awaited me without her. By crying, I gave the court the satisfaction of appearing remorseful. Everyone loves remorse. "I can see you are remorseful for your crime, Mr. Ascher," said Judge Poliakoff, the tiny judge with the cherry lipstick who suddenly sounded gentle. "Before I sentence you, is there anything you wish to say to the court at this time? Stand if you wish to speak to the court."

I stood up and spoke to the courtroom for the first time. "Ladies and gentlemen," I started, thinking that one does not address a court as if he were giving a valedictory address. "People." That didn't sound right either but I continued. "I'm sorry. I'm not sorry for the crime because I committed no crime. I'm sorry that someone hasn't gone out to find the real killer. I'm sorry that you think I would have killed my wife. I loved my wife. We argued, yes, but who in here—"

"Mr. Ascher!" the judge interjected, and not gently. "You are not to argue your case! Your case has been decided! Decided! You have murdered an innocent woman, the most important person in your life, a woman expecting her first child and yours too! Do you have anything mitigating to say before tomorrow's sentencing?"

Everyone was taken aback by the scolding she had given me; I had never heard such palpable silence. From this silence came a sound, the unmistakable sound of the magazine editor's emery board. The scraping so unnerved me that when I looked at the judge's bodiless face and bouffant, I gave in to an irresistible urge to laugh. I imagined her as Senor Wences' hand puppet, Johnnie. The judge stared incredulously, shaking her head. "Sorry, Your Honor. Did you say 'mitigating'?" I had regained control but too late. "Your Honor, ladies and gentlemen of the jury, I'm a good person. I'm also a bad person. Just as good or bad as any of you. I'm flawed but so is everyone else. But I would never kill anyone, especially someone I loved."

"Very well, Mr. Ascher," said the tiny judge whose cherry red lipstick was now smeared above the top lip as if she had licked it with her tongue. Licked it as if she was sealing an envelope but missed. Her *very well* indicated that my rhetorical flourish had been wasted, that I had failed to mitigate. Aside from being irked by my laughter at such a solemn moment, the judge was obviously disappointed that I hadn't taken responsibility for the crime.

Next, she asked Marsha's father for a victim impact statement. Her mother, Mrs. Gorstein-Hirsch, had already decided not to speak. The year between the killing and the trial must not have made her suffering any easier to bear. Mr. Hirsch stood solemnly before the witness chair.

"Losing a child, a daughter, is the worst thing that can happen to a person…"

As he spoke, I thought that losing a wife is every bit as bad. But the court had spoken. I hadn't lost Marsha. I'd killed her. I wasn't the aggrieved husband; I was the cause of Mr. Hirsch's grief.

"How can I say what Marsha meant to us? This man sitting in front of you, this Mr. Ascher, who we gave our love to and welcomed into our home, has torn a vital organ from my body. He has reached inside me and cut out my heart." All this was said as he tried to suppress deep sobs, although I, thinking of the very same Marsha, couldn't suppress mine. "And she was going to bring a new life into our lives. She was just so happy and now she's dead, murdered. Justice is a small compensation for what we've lost. It's small but it's all we have. Now Mr. Ascher is sorry. You can see he's sorry. But it's too late. Your Honor and members of the jury, he should be locked up forever, and throw away the key."

Next day, the jury unanimously recommended to the judge that I be given life in prison without the possibility of parole, or *life without*, as prisoners call it. This tiny, young-looking judge who may have been a lot older than she looked, who I thought, being a woman, might rise above vindictiveness and give me a chance for parole, said first that I was "an amoral individual who has no regard for the sanctity of human life." I'd heard that phrase describing psychopaths and their ilk many times before, and now it was being applied to me. The judge then said that I would be going to prison for the rest of my natural life. What should I have expected after laughing at her face? What does it mean—your natural life? Does that mean I have a supernatural life somewhere in a parallel universe ruled by a loving God? She might just have said, *You'll be in prison, Mr. Ascher, until the day you die, until the day you drop dead.* Like Rufus Bass. Six years in the banking industry—imagine calling that an industry—trying for all six years to behave like a white man and then killing two co-workers in a senseless rampage, dropping dead of heart failure at the age of forty-four on his way out to the prison yard.

I told a guard going out on break that Rufus might be having a heart attack. I pointed to where he was being supported by two other inmates. The guard looked doubtful, probably thinking that forty-four year old men do not have heart attacks. He popped out a package of Tums, only three Tums remaining in the roll, passed it through the fence and went on his way. Rufus was not, however, suffering from indigestion. When I turned back, he was lying stretched out on the dusty ground, his face now turned a paler shade of black. An inmate started banging his chest like a jackhammer. Having been a cabbie, I knew CPR. I pushed the other prisoner aside and began my work. In time, maybe a couple of minutes, Rufus's eyes opened. Jesus, I'd saved him! At that moment, a selfish thought flashed through my head: *Maybe now they'll give me a shot at parole.* But he shook his head a couple of times. I knew what he meant. He shook his head and closed his eyes, this time for good. Given the chance, I'd have done the same.

My conviction was wrongful but it served a purpose. If they couldn't find the actual killer, better that they found the wrong person—better *that* than no person at all. I could suffer for another person's crime and bring some measure of peace to the Hirsches and to the community. My life would at least have a purpose, but not to me.

O

Three times a day, just in case someone has escaped or is escaping, every inmate in this place is counted. No one I've met at the prison can remember an escape. Nevertheless. Nevertheless. All over America, in every single prison, the prisoners are counted three times a day to make sure that they're all present. If they've died during the past three and a half hours, they are no longer present but they are still counted; they are counted until the relatives come to claim the body or they are lowered into the crowded hole at the rear of the prison.

If I don't outlive them, my mother and father will not be claiming me unless they have a change of heart, maybe heart transplants, so that they have hearts of flesh and not of stone. They came to visit me at the hell of Rikers Island before I was sent upstate. They loved Marsha and were looking forward to being grandparents, rolling a stroller through the park, spoiling our child. They knew that Marsha and I were experiencing problems but they never thought it would end like this.

I tried to speak sense to them. "Of course we had problems. Who doesn't? You have problems."

"Not like your problems, Joel."

"Mom, you argue about everything. Where to buy toilet paper. Where to—"

"We always go to Costco for that stuff. Why would we argue over that?"

"It was a figure of speech."

"A figure of speech?"

"No, maybe not a figure of speech. An exaggeration. A joke." What the hell was it?

"A joke? This is a joke? Murdering your wife is a joke?" I felt like a boy in the principal's office.

"Mel, calm down. Don't forget that Pearlstone diagnosed him with Asperger's."

"Asperger's," he sneered.

"That's why he's inappropriate. That's why he can't get a decent job. That's why Pearlstone referred him to a specialist when he was five years old."

"Pearlstone is an old man," I said. "And a prick to boot."

"He could see you were conflicted."

"'He could see', Jesus H. Christ! I told him I was conflicted!"

"You hear that?" my mother asked my father. Then she said to me, "You're a powder keg."

"Dad, I tell you that I'm innocent." My father just had to believe me.

"Say what you want, Joel, but the verdict was guilty."

"Dad!"

"In our legal system, that means you're guilty." A cockroach on a mistimed outing swung up from below the tabletop and began moving cautiously across the table. I stubbed the roach out with my thumb.

"Oh my God!" my mother said.

To no one at all, I said, "I feel like I'm living in some Kafka novel."

"Kafka? This isn't Kafka, Joel. It's more like Beckett. Wouldn't you say it was more like Beckett, Deb?"

"*Waiting for Godot*?"

"More like *Endgame*." My father stroked his silver goatee. He is an English prof, a university professor of English who is worshipped by his female students and so will never retire. He met my mother in graduate school where they smoked pot and dropped acid. I grew up with them on a commune. My memory from that time is fuzzy, but Mel and Debra told me they left because people wouldn't pick up after themselves. My brother, Ed, was born three years later, after we'd moved to the suburbs.

During my adolescence, I got into Jimmy Page and Pink Floyd and never looked forward again. I didn't complete my education. I never wanted a nine to five job. Ask me what I was doing before driving a cab and I'll tell you that I ate, slept, and listened to music, especially "Stairway to Heaven," several times a day. Listening to "Stairway to Heaven" was the one thing I did more than jerking off.

Late one Saturday afternoon—I was nineteen at the time—my friend Bob and I were listening full volume to "Stairway to Heaven." My father went down to the basement and flipped off the fuse connected to my bedroom. The turntable, sounding like a large zipper, ground to a halt. My father banged on the door but, in our paranoid frame of mind, we thought it was the police. The banging continued along with a loud, "Open up!" which I dimly realized might be my father.

When I opened the door, he burst inside, red-faced, spitting and screaming, "Enough! I've had enough of this! You," meaning Bob, "get the fuck out!" Bob left and never came over again. My father moved toward the turntable but I blocked his path. That seemed to restore his sanity. "You couldn't hear an air-raid siren with that noise." He opened the window and waved the smoke from the room. Smoldering with rage, his voice choked, he said, "Take a shower and get dressed. We're going to the opera." Shocked into sobriety, my face must have registered the look of a youthful offender who had just received the death penalty. "You heard me." I thought of standing my ground as an independent nineteen-year old, a voter and a legal drinker, but I lacked a track record of responsible behavior. I took another tack instead.

"Why should I take Mom's ticket?"

"Deb hates Wagner. He was an anti-Semite."

"Well, I don't like him either."

"Shut up. You never even heard of him." That was true. Given my father's level of anger, I thought the better of refusing.

My father looked the other way when I came down dressed in black jeans and a Led Zeppelin shirt. He knew enough to quit while he was ahead, so he just had to endure the haughty stares directed at me in the French restaurant and in the Met lobby. At dinner, I ordered some pricey hors d'oeuvre and lobster thermidor. My real revenge was going to take place at the opera where I had every intention of falling asleep. As we took our seats in the dress circle, the candelabras rose past us to the top of the auditorium. A short pudgy smiling man with a halo of wiry hair, a man whom I was later to meet, emerged from a hole underneath the stage and bowed to wild applause.

Out of silence and darkness, a rumble came up from the orchestra pit and swelled into something impossible, something ineffable. "Dad, what is that?" I loudly whispered.

"Shhhh."

Listening to the growing volume and the swirling themes, I began to tremble and cry, but I felt no joy or sorrow. I was being lifted from my life into a place I thought that only I could understand. I looked to my right and saw my father wiping tears from his face. If only I had reached out and touched him. I never even thanked him for changing my life.

"That's good, Mel. *Endgame.*"

"Haven't you heard of wrongful convictions, Dad? Of DNA exonerations?"

"On television maybe."

"Dad, I would never kill Marsha. You know that. You have to believe me." I was running out of breath.

It was time for my mother to start in on me. Debra is a tall, well-dressed woman—even to the point of wearing pompoms on her tennis shoes—whose eyes are shaded by dark glasses and a visor, even indoors, because of some eye condition. She always looks as if she's headed on or off a private golf course. One thing she doesn't look like is a hippie, former or otherwise. "Why couldn't you get a better lawyer, Joel?"

"I like Fiedler."

"You like him because he doesn't cost a lot."

"That's not true. I like him because he's a *mensch*. And I'm a big case for him. Expensive lawyers don't give you the attention that Fiedler does."

"Who needs his attention? You're in prison for life."

"He looks like a rat," my father said.

"Maybe so."

"Where did you find him?"

"I'll have you know he came highly recommended." They stared at me, waiting no doubt to hear who recommended Fiedler. I wasn't about to tell them. "All right. He may not be a great lawyer."

"No question about it," my mother said. "I have to deal with lawyers all the time. I know good lawyers from shysters."

"Who cares if he's a shyster? That's not the issue," my father said. "He should have known that Pearlstone was going to blindside him. Joel, Fiedler is incompetent. Any good lawyer would have found out about Pearlstone."

"That's just stupid, Dad."

Looking at my mother, he said, "You're right. He can't read people. Pearlstone was right about the Asperger's."

They began to machine gun me with criticism. First my mother: "I can't get over the fact that he testified against you. Your own doctor."

My father: "Like a priest revealing what's said in confession."

My mother: "You've got to have a guilty conscience to hire a lawyer like that."

"Would the both of you just shut up! Shut up! Where the hell were you for most of the trial? The so-called trial."

My father maintained his calm. "You've always had a quick temper, Joel. You've always simmered."

My mother interjected, "I told you he's a powder keg."

As if to confirm their assessment of me, my anger continued to spill over. "You didn't even come to the sentencing!"

"Can you understand how painful it is to have our names in the papers, on television, everywhere we look? To see you escorted down the hallway by a phalanx of policemen and know that our son is being looked at by millions of people? Can you understand what that means? To have neighbors refuse to speak to us?" What my father said was true. What was I thinking? That being sentenced to life in prison was some kind of university commencement exercise?

My mother cried out, "We may have to change our names!"

"Debra, we already had this out. Am I going to walk into class and suddenly be professor John Doe?"

"Who said anything about John Doe?"

I had to take control of myself and the situation. This time I spoke calmly to both of them. "You don't seriously believe that I killed Marsha, do you?"

"I don't know what to believe. What do you believe, Deb?"

"Bottom line, Mom," I said. "Can you believe that your son, that I, a gentle, peace loving man, would do such a thing? You know it's not possible."

"The verdict was guilty. What do I know?" My mother was in tears. "They said you were guilty."

"I was *found* guilty, Mom."

"Which," my father added, "means you've lost your innocence."

He had a point. It's hard to argue with university academics. Especially when you're a cab driver, maybe an intellectual type of cab driver, but lacking the polish of a Ph.D., in other words, a vast disappointment to them. Marsha, on the other hand, was in her third year of law school. She was the apple of their eye—of their eyes.

"Dad, the system allows for appeals. Even the system recognizes that mistakes are made."

Both my parents held their heads in their hands with this gesture of Job's despair and—what else—disgust, perplexity at what God had done to them.

I looked around the crowded cafeteria. African Americans, Hispanics, a smattering of whites, girlfriends, wives, grandparents, small children, even babies made up the crowd. The prisoners have to sit on the chair marked with yellow tape after checking in with the soon-to-be-pensioned guard reading the porn magazine. These other families are loyal families even though most of the prisoners are guilty of crimes. No matter the weekend, the Rikers cafeteria is crowded with visitors, unlike the upstate prison where they wound up sending me. When the conversation fell silent, my parents kept looking around the cafeteria. Both were appalled and couldn't wait to leave.

My younger brother Ed came in for an obligatory visit the day before they shipped me upstate. Ed is emaciated, you might say skeletal. He suffers from an eating disorder. I can barely look at him. Because I'd been defined as a murderer, he couldn't look at me either.

"I can't believe what's happened, Joel. The ground is opening up and swallowing our family."

Yes, I thought, we're all dying of a wrongful conviction. "I am innocent, Ed. You can believe me on that. Brother to brother. I need someone to believe in me and that has to be you."

"It's been a year from hell." He started shaking his head. "You can see I look like hell."

"Yes."

"I have to get away. I don't know anymore. I have to get away."

"What a mess. I've made a mess. I'm sorry, Ed. I'm sorry."

"I wish I knew what to do." His head was still shaking back and forth.

"You can help me get through this, Ed. Pay the lawyer. Make sure I have some cash on hand and some decent food."

"I wish I could help you there, brother. I really do. I've been short the last three months. They've cut back my hours; I'm in the next wave to be laid off." My brother, Ed, my younger brother, assumed the same position that my parents had the day before. He held his head in his hands, hands the light could pass through—what's the word—translucent, translucent hands, like bone china. "If it wasn't for Mom and Dad, I couldn't even pay the rent."

"Ed, I spoke to the bank before the trial. I told them to give you signing privileges on my account. In case I was convicted. It's now a joint account."

"It is?" He looked up.

"All you need to do is sign the papers. I'm going to need you to pay for my expenses from that account. Fiedler, maybe a private eye, whatever is needed."

"Hire a dick?"

"Dick? Yes, I suppose. A dick."

"You can count on me for that."

"I know I can." I was bribing him, bribing my own brother. The bribe was translucent—no, transparent.

"You'll win your appeal, Joel."

"I hope so."

He took hold of my arm and stared straight into my eyes. "I'll be standing outside the prison on the day you get out. We'll hug. We'll cry together. It's a fucking injustice what's happened to you."

"Thanks, Ed. You don't know what it means to me to have you on my side."

O

What I should have said to them, what I know now, is that the whole and only purpose of the appeals system, of the whole corrections system, is to keep lawyers and judges busy, to keep guards walking and searching for drugs and weapons in inmates' anuses, and to make sure that the traffic coming into the prisons is a lot heavier than the traffic coming out—a hundred lanes going in to one lane going out—and, of course, to distribute tax money. Even prisoners get in on this money. Some of them return to prison deliberately, committing flagrant misdemeanors, if business gets slow on the street.

How depressing it all is, how grinding and purposeless. Right now, I could shout out my innocence but no one outside or inside the prison will either hear me or care. And something terrible is happening as well. Doubt has begun to gnaw—the squirrel of doubt. What gnaws on this earth? What large or small rodent? I can't even remember that anymore, although only mammals gnaw, or maybe carpenter ants, judging from the piles of sawdust. Dogs gnaw on bones. Chipmunks. Chipmunks of doubt are gnawing. Maybe I did black out and act under some unconscious compulsion and maybe, perhaps, just possibly killed my wife. How can anyone know such a thing? Maybe they know more than I do? Did I have reason to kill Marsha? Would I have gained any advantage? Did I need her money? No. Did she cheat on me? Probably not, although that Thad guy, or was it Skip, maybe Chip or Tim—he had a name like a cartoon squirrel—something like that, anyway, she seemed to like him a little. Maybe she liked him a lot. I could see why, why she would stare at a lithe looking guy like that in line at a movie theatre; the fact that she knew him and I didn't was cause for concern. But so what? I am not, nor was not, even before my re-definition as a murderer, a jealous man. True, I may have a quick temper. True too that I may have dressed with a certain carelessness, fallen a little to seed for a thirty-six year old, become less sexually desirable and maybe more vulnerable to cheating by a beautiful wife. I wonder if pregnant women cheat? Maybe the first trimester is the best time to cheat? Jesus, what a thought! Since learning she was pregnant, I lost interest in how I looked in front of a mirror. It wasn't good—how I looked in front of a mirror whenever I cared to look—especially that ring above my hips, at the center of which a fungus grows. How could she have loved me? And yet she did. She said she did and I believe what she said until this day. And how I regret not loving her back, no, I regret not showing her that I loved her back. Maybe since I never saw my parents do it, I didn't think it was necessary.

The only time I came out of myself was at work. I was one of those cab drivers who, contrary to training, never shuts up. I was told very clearly by my cigar-chomping boss, a guy who looked like a caricature of Danny DeVito, that a cab driver is nothing but *a means a' conveyance*, not a friend of his passengers. A *means a' conveyance*! I was also warned to speak only if the passenger spoke to me and only on the subject, with the sole exception of the weather, initiated by the passenger. So I became a means of conveyance that spoke only about weather—for less than a day.

I drove at night, the late night fares being more interesting than the daytime businessmen. I felt so free! I had some great and talented people in my cab. Opera stars. Leontyne Price, retired but regal, René Fleming, James Levine, rotund, brilliant, ebullient, and garrulous. How I love using words like that, words you'd be killed for using inside a prison! Joseph Papp rode with me, Bill T. Jones, city politicians too, crooks of the first order. I know opera, theatre, dance, and politics. I read *The New York Times* and *The New Yorker*. I did the crosswords. I know sports as well as any New Yorker. I drove Oscar De La Hoya, Hurricane Carter, Jason Giambi, and a crazy but very nice hockey player from a place called Medicine Hat. Medicine Hat. What a great name for a city! I think I drove a Knick, an Italian named Gamberini or something, so tall he could barely fit through the door and had to lean over for the entire trip. I could engage all of them knowledgeably and still get them where they wanted to go. I drove fast but never recklessly. I knew when to take the staggered lights up Third Avenue; knew when to take the FDR Drive; and knew when to ride with the staggered lights down Second Avenue. Ditto the West Side. Mel and Debra were unimpressed by my career, but Marsha never tired of my stories, especially the one about James Levine.

Of course it was Levine who was conducting *Das Rheingold* when I first went to the Met with my father. I picked him up in Chelsea on his way to Lincoln Center and recognized him immediately. He was already in pretty bad shape, so I got out and helped him into the cab while he grimaced in pain. He was grateful that I recognized him and liked it even more when I praised his work.

"You produce beautiful sounds from the orchestra and your singers are in love with you. I'd do anything to have your talent, Jimmy." I wanted to show him I was familiar with what insiders called him but, just in case, I added "Maestro."

"You don't want to live anyone else's life, my friend, least of all, mine. I can see you're a good cab driver."

"Yeah. Yeah, I know."

"Talent is relative to what you do. My philosophy is *Do what you do well*. It comes with knowing who you are and believing in yourself. Nothing should get in the way of that belief. I tell that to singers and musicians all the time."

"I would love to conduct an opera orchestra. Just once. I'd love to get swept away like that."

"Have you been able to catch a Met performance?"

"Many times, Maestro Levine. My wife and I."

"Next time you're up there and I'm working, ask an usher to see me backstage."

"Thank you, Maestro." His invitation was exciting, although I was secretly hoping to be invited to a rehearsal.

"I see your name is Joel, Joel Ascher." He pulled out a card and wrote my name down.

Making headway of any sort with a man of his stature made me anxious. I don't function well when I'm anxious. "I've seen you conduct many times. Your *Boccanegra* is the second best in the world."

"Next to whom, Joel?" he asked, slightly less affable.

"Abbado. But he doesn't quite have your sweep, your grandeur. What he has is pacing."

I could see he didn't take that awfully well either. I mean the comment about pacing, even if that's true.

"You know," I continued, "it's the same with Wagner. I've often wondered why you take Wagner's music so slowly. Have you listened to Solti? What a *Ring*! What drive! Bruno Walter too. Your *Ring* cycle, it's lush, yes, very lush, but a little slow for my taste."

Silence. Once again, the report card flashed in front of my face. No matter. I kept on going. "Is it because you love that beautiful music so much, those big sounds, that you sacrifice the drama?"

The traffic on 8th Avenue had stalled. Levine said, "You can let me out right here." Passing the fare and, to his credit, an ample tip through the plastic divider, he struggled out the door into the middle of Port Authority traffic, cane and all. He looked back inside before closing the door, "My friend, stick to driving cabs," hailing another cab with his cane. The honking was cacophonous.

Maybe Pearlstone knew what he was talking about? I think I really do have Asperger's. Mild Asperger's, although mild is bad enough. But I did too well for myself to have serious Asperger's. Or maybe I don't really have Asperger's. Maybe I'm just offensive or socially stupid. One of my girlfriends in high school—all right, I had one girlfriend in high school, Tanya, who dropped me one week into our relationship—told me that I was the dumbest smart person she ever met.

Cab driving is not just a lark; the field has a lot of emotional wear and tear, attempted robberies, fares that don't pay, and all sorts of hysterical people. I cleared nine hundred dollars a week, twelve hundred during holidays, not enough, of course, to afford a condo in Manhattan. That I owe to online poker. When it comes to poker, I'm an *idiot savant*. There are millions of ignorant young people out there, living with their parents, throwing away the family's money online, money I was only too happy to relieve them of. Because of poker, I didn't need the money from cab driving anymore. What I needed were people I didn't know, people to entertain through a rear-view mirror. The poker paid off the loan for my medallion and allowed us to move from Queens to the Upper East Side.

O

The *day of*, a Sunday, I was in The Village, shopping for rare records. I went to Regeneration Vinyl, but I couldn't find the live *Traviata* sung by Maria Callas.

I picked up the *Sunday Times*, had a coffee and read for a while. By the time I started back home, it was New York hot, humid, slimy, and filthy. All I could think of was getting home and having a shower, but, in every aspect, it was not to be a lucky day. The train got stuck inside the tunnel at 12:45. Near 2 p.m., just before the dozen or so passengers, maybe MacSweeney amongst them, were baked to death, they marched us down the track to the next platform, the Union Square station. Disgusting! Norway rats as big as small dogs scurried around the tracks. This incident was confirmed in the courtroom, all except my being on the subway.

I emerged from hell on wheels into hell on earth and caught the first cab that, given the way I looked, kindly stopped for me. I thanked God out loud that the cab was air-conditioned. Cabs are air-conditioned by law but that law is followed more in the breach or is it honored in the breach? I think Hamlet says that or maybe Macbeth. I got out of the air-conditioned cab in front of my Upper East Side apartment. I don't know who the cab driver was—I normally look at the ID—but I was too traumatized by the experience in the subway tunnel. I exchanged a few mindless words with Carlos the doorman, noticing that because of the heat he was out of livery, and walked to the elevator.

Every prisoner, the guilty or the innocent, never stops thinking of the day of his arrest, the signals missed, the mistakes made that placed him inside the walls of a prison. I should have looked to see who that cab driver was. I should have spoken to the record store proprietor. I should have done a lot of things differently. The one thing I did do was look at my watch. It was 2:44 when I emerged from the cab, thinking that Marsha would be worried. When I entered our apartment, right away I felt that something was wrong. I sensed an intruder. I spoke out Marsha's name while standing frozen in the foyer. Then I moved toward the bedroom, one step at a time, as if I was walking in the dark without a flashlight. I found Marsha turned on her side, sleeping in the way she usually does, but for the fact that it was in the middle of a

Sunday afternoon. A pile of law books and what I saw to be an eviscerated copy of the Constitution were spread on the bed and around the floor in haphazard fashion. Since her pregnancy had moved into the second trimester, she had been complaining about the fatigue she felt while studying the law. I was certain that she had thrown the books aside and gone to sleep, certain except for that sense I still had, that sense of an intruder. As I looked at her, I noticed that the top sheet was rumpled. I touched her with my left hand and then shook her. No response. I climbed on to the bed beside her, looked over her shoulder and saw that the half moon of her face was pale, pale as, well, the moon. My right hand on the bed felt sticky. I raised my hand to my face. It was red. I thought that if I got off the bed, turned around, went back out the door and came back in again, that this might go away. I didn't do that though, and it wouldn't have helped if I had. I turned Marsha over and saw the handle of a knife, the very knife I had used to cut up fruit that morning and left in the sink, protruding from her chest. That was *fact* and I was...unprepared—no, that's not the right word—I've never found the word to describe the way I felt. I know I had momentarily stopped breathing.

I stood up and immediately fell over. I crawled to the telephone and tried to call 911, but my hand was sweating and quivering to such an extent that I couldn't hold the receiver steady. What else could I have done at that moment? Start banging on doors? The widow in the apartment across the hall was almost ninety and the news might have killed her. Hell, it might have killed her if she looked at me in my condition. I didn't know others on the floor except to say hello on the elevator or hold the door while they threw their garbage down the chute. How would I feel if one of them came to me and said they had found a murdered spouse lying on the bed? So I picked up the phone again, breathed deeply and carefully pressed 911. The woman answering the call was well trained in calming people down and getting information.

I waited until I heard the sirens and took the elevator down to meet the police at the door. Carlos, the doorman out of livery, was talking to one of them when I got down to the lobby. He pointed me out. I must have looked positively feral by then.

"What's your name by the way?" the cop asked him.

"Carlos Estevez."

"Spell that for me." He wrote the name on his pad. "Don't go anywhere. We're going to need to ask you some questions later. Think about who you saw going in and out of here today. If you saw anyone you couldn't recognize."

Carlos began to speak. "I don't think—"

"Look, just give it some thought. Whatever or whoever you saw that was out of the ordinary."

"Ascher?" The policeman, Captain Swain, the barber pole with the red face and the white hair—a high rent district cop wearing a cop hat, a white shirt and tie—looked at me as if he was seeing a madman, a madman, he immediately suspected, who had just murdered his wife. Swain was accompanied by a uniformed cop. Then another car pulled up aggressively at the curbside. I saw three more uniformed cops jump out of this car as if they were running in to prevent a bank robbery. An ambulance was next. Sirens. Lights. Shouting. Hubbub. People returning with baguettes sticking out of shopping bags stopped to look.

"Joel Ascher. Yes, that's me." Four cops, all wearing bulletproof vests, were soon surrounding me; it felt as if they were staring down, even though they might not have been as tall as I was. Along with Swain, they radiated authority and physical power. I thought at the time that it must be really hot inside those dark uniforms and bulletproof vests. But I was the one sweating in my checked cotton short-sleeved shirt.

Swain continued. "Is that A…S…H…E…R?"

"No, it's with a 'C'." I wanted to start off on the right foot. I wanted them to know I would tell the truth.

"'C'? A...C...H...E...R?"

Carlos held the door for the ambulance paramedics, one holding a metal box. Two other paramedics wheeling in a bed with straps came through while Carlos still held the door.

"Hold it one second!" the captain ordered the paramedics.

"No, it's A...S...C...H...E...R."

After the captain wrote my name properly, he looked me in the eyes. His stare was penetrating, a trained stare, no doubt. "Take us upstairs," the captain ordered me. I thought for a moment that I'd left my keys in the apartment but realized that I hadn't worn a jacket that day. Still, it took me a long time to get them out of my pocket. My nerves were as tight as my pants.

"Calm down, Mr. Ascher." The captain put a steadying hand on my shoulder. As always in New York, people, even little twin girls in pinafores, continued to stare rudely and listen in. Casual passersby, seeing all the activity, came into the building. Carlos made no attempt to stop them. The city of theatre was having a free show.

"When we get upstairs, Mr. Ascher, stand outside in the hallway." I began to feel as if I'd done something terribly wrong. The captain held out his hand and I dropped the keys on his palm. The crowd kept gawking. Along with the heat, suspicion drifted into the lobby through the open doors of the building.

On the elevator, crushed in by Swain, four cops and four paramedics with a bed, I felt I needed to say something, something to take control of my situation. "Whatever you want me to do. I'll call her family...I'll—"

"You do what we tell you to do. That'll make it easier for you."

I was plastered up to the elevator mirror. My face was blanched. Ghastly. My checked cotton short-sleeve shirt was soaked. The elevator was packed shoulder to shoulder like the subway at five o'clock on a weekday, which, thank God, I didn't usually have to endure. A two hundred and fifty pound African American cop leaned heavily on me, I think deliberately. Male sweat permeated. Latex gloves were snapped on.

I waited in the hallway with the big, impassive African American cop, my apartment door propped open. Doubtless, the paramedics were trying to get vital signs from Marsha. One of the beat cops came out shaking his head. "She's long gone. When did you find her?"

"Just before."

The elevator disgorged another contingent, two more detectives in white shirtsleeves and ties along with a crime scene photographer and a TV news anchorwoman.

The detectives snapped on latex gloves and brushed past me into the apartment. The photographer followed behind them. "I think she's pregnant, at least she *was*," I heard someone shout, likely one of the paramedics.

The captain stepped outside the apartment.

"We've got the cameras set up outside, Captain," said the anchorwoman.

"That's good, Carrie, we'll be out there right away." Hearing this, Carrie walked over to the elevator.

To me, Swain said, "We're calling the coroner. That's your wife, right?"

I nodded.

"Your wife is dead."

"I gathered."

"You gathered? What's the matter with you, Mr. Ascher? That's your wife in there and she was pregnant."

"I know. I know."

"Was that *your* baby inside her?"

"I hope so. I mean—" What did I mean?

"Mr. Ascher, under the circumstances, I would have thought you'd be more emotional."

"I must be in shock." But I thought he was right. I wasn't feeling anything but numb.

The detectives stepped outside the apartment. "Let's take Mr. Ascher in for further questioning," said the captain. To me he said flatly, "It's routine. I'm sorry we have to do this at such a difficult time."

As I emerged from the building, a large crowd of people had gathered out front. The anchorwoman, Carrie, shoved a microphone into my face as the cameramen focused their lenses on me. I'd seen her on TV, *MY9* or some other trashy news show. She must have asked me some insensitive question, but I couldn't hear it and, even if I did, was not in any shape to respond. "Oh, the power of one 911 call," I thought, "that could set into motion this whole network of people!"

O

"What we have here, ladies and gentlemen of the jury, is an ironclad case of spousal murder. It happens every day and it happens everywhere. The defendant degraded and abused Marsha, his wife, in public. He feared that his life of selfish indulgence would be destroyed by Marsha's having a child. He entered the bedroom brandishing a knife while she was still asleep. Marsha came awake and they struggled briefly before the defendant plunged the kitchen knife into her chest, snuffing out the life of his loving spouse and the future life inside her. Then, in a moment of remorse for what he'd done, he placed the sheet back on top of her. What we know for certain is that there were signs of a struggle but no signs of a break-in, that there were no other fingerprints on the knife aside from the defendant's, that the defendant had Marsha's blood on his right hand and on his clothing and that he showed no emotional attachment to her when questioned by the police."

Alpha/Brookes then made his characteristic gesture, his hand passing through his amply greased head. He made it appear that he was choked up, playing at sorrow and doing a good job of it. As I glanced sideways at Fiedler, I could see the hint of a confident smile on my lawyer's face. As to where he got his confidence, it puzzles me to this day.

"Did our defendant take responsibility for the savage killing? No, he did not! With great deviousness, the defendant left the apartment. Unbeknownst to him, he was seen by a young woman on the way out. My learned colleague claims that the doorman didn't identify his client leaving the building. But the doorman told you he wasn't sure that he saw the defendant. Maybe that would suffice as reasonable doubt were it not for all the other evidence. Remember too that our witness had *no* doubt that she saw Mr. Ascher and, indeed, was able to describe the defendant's clothes and demeanor on that fatal day.

"The defendant tells us that he went searching for a rare opera record earlier on that morning…" and so on, piling shovelfuls of dirt on me until the real me was no longer visible. I'll be damned if I didn't believe him myself. By any objective assessment, I was damned. The Christian Hell's Angel stared at me as if he wanted to escort me on the back of his motorcycle into the very fires of damnation. Yes, I could see that he did believe in retribution.

Fiedler leaned over and whispered in my ear: "Anyone can see that Brookes is embellishing."

"The defendant told the police that he'd been stuck on the subway. My learned colleague tells you that his client could not possibly have known by then that the subway had been stuck that morning. But we showed you that radio and television reports of the power failure in the subway began a mere half hour after the incident began.

"What really happened was that one hour and forty-five minutes after he'd plunged the knife into Marsha's chest, the defendant returned home from wherever he'd hidden, making sure this time to converse with the doorman. He went upstairs and pretended to discover Marsha's body. He called 911…"

"Poppycock," whispered Fiedler.

"Finally, you heard the defendant's confession. He admitted the possibility that he had murdered Marsha. You can draw your own conclusions about what he meant by his statement." Alpha/Brookes had played that confession *ad nauseam* in court; that didn't stop him from doing it again.

So you say it was possible that you killed Marsha?

Sure. I told you. And who knows who else I killed?

"Objection!" cried Fiedler, reflexively, looking for some advantage. The court waited to hear his objection but he just stood there pathetically.

O

I'm on a train, a quaintly decorated train from the 1920's or 30's, a train that is going a long distance, built for comfort. It looks like the train from *The Sting*, red velvet seats, tablecloths, porters, waiters. True to the film set, I enter a private coach and interrupt a card game. Poker. Five card sharks sit at a table. A man resembling Robert Redford looks up at me, while the Robert Shaw figure shoots me a poisonous glance. I look for Paul Newman. Too bad, he isn't there. I'd love to have told him how much I enjoyed *Cool Hand Luke*. Two others are wearing visors and smoking. I think happily that I'm in a movie until I recognize my faded lawyer. My faded lawyer with the same worn-out blue suit, snowflakes on the shoulders, does not have a visor. He doesn't have a good hand either. Ten high. Ten fucking high. But he's betting an awful lot of money. He turns to me and winks. Does he really think he's got the best hand? "Don't," I want to say, but I can't speak. I would have folded this hand right at the start. Four of clubs and a ten of diamonds in the hole. The stakes keep increasing; ten high is not going to cut it. I'm choking. The cigarette smoke is choking me.

"Huel," I hear. "Huel." Hernandez shakes me awake like a rag doll. He's a powerful man although only five foot seven. I'm coughing and so is he. "I think you maybe dying." His coughs are very deep.

"No such luck."

"Maybe. Maybe you have a heart attack—like Rufus. You know they poison Rufus."

"If they did, they did him a favor."

"They poison everyone in here. *Todo el mundo*. Soon we all be dead."

"No, that's unlikely."

"They want to get rid of us."

You had to start worrying when Hernandez started going off like this. "Have you taken your pills?"

"Maybe not."

"Take them, Victor. It wouldn't hurt."

"Maybe I don't wake up. They poison them too."

It was time to use reason. "Victor, listen to me—"

"They poison everything. The water."

"Victor! You want to know why they won't poison us?" He stares at me as if he's just noticed I was in the cell with him, even though he's been talking to me the whole time. I think they put me in his cell to drive *me* crazy. "We're their bread and butter. You get it?" He continues to stare blankly. "*Pan y mantequilla. Estamos pan y mantequilla.*" Jesus, his English is way better than my Spanish.

"*Pan y mantequilla?*" The metaphor—or is it an idiom—doesn't work for him.

"*Dinero!* We are money to them. Jobs. *Napanoch*, all of New York State would be dead without us. *Morte.*"

"*Morte.*"

I can see that my efforts are causing even more consternation. "Victor, take your pills."

He continues to stare. I try again: "*Un prison sin hombres esta una escuela sin muchachos.*"

"*Muchachos,*" he says, laughing. "*Muchachos!*"

"Okay, *estudiantes.*"

Shaking his head, he jumps down, reaches under the bed and hands me a package. My name is on the package.

"When did this come?"

"Williams. While you was sleeping."

I rip it open. Good old Williams. Lamisil, tea tree oil, and floss—two flosses.

O

The stone, steel and wire that encase my body are meant to keep me away from the civilization outside the prison. My prison is located near Kingston, New York, in a countryside I can never see; the windows of a prison allow no view except for a slice of sky. The killer can see the flowers and the trees. Birds are out there too; sometimes I can hear them. The world just outside the prison, the world of Nature as it's called, the world that civilized people live in but don't respect, the world where I could lie in the shade in the cool grass is there for her killer but not for me. One go-around is all a person gets, and I don't even get to live my own life.

When four other convicts and I were approaching this institution in the back of a barred school bus, one of the guards told me, "Take a good look at your new home, offender Ascher, because you're never going to see it again from the outside." My new home, as he called it, an outsized building, had no business being in this poor innocuous place. My mouth must have hung open because the same guard could not repress his laughter. The front of the prison appeared to be half a mile wide and was flanked by two thick turrets, a medieval castle in the middle of upstate New York and me headed for the dungeon to do time.

I am doing time, so they say, but, in reality, time is undoing me. All of humanity serves Father Time until Father Time dies with the last of humanity. I am serving *life without*, but, in reality, *life without* is life without life. Long ago, they abandoned the death penalty in New York. I am serving the life penalty, otherwise known as mercy. Those of us serving *life without* are boiled, pickled and served up to the Grim Reaper who deposits us back into eternity.

I spend a good bit of time every day overdosing on thought, trying to work out conundrums, and just as much time thinking about my case. I keep thinking that there's a key, an aha moment, a sudden insight that will make sense of what happened that day and will reveal why I am in this place. When I find the key, I will know the *WHO* and the *WHY*, who killed Marsha and why. Everything will fall into place and I will be free.

What had happened that Sunday? True, there was sign of a struggle but not a great struggle. The sheet was rumpled but not extremely so. Maybe she knew her assailant and let him into the apartment? Robbery was certainly not the motive. Nothing was disturbed, nothing taken. In fact, one hundred and sixty-five dollars and a good wristwatch were left inside my night table drawer.

Fiedler tells me that even if things were taken, money or iPods or cell phones or BlackBerrys or CD players, even if things went missing, the police would say that the killer wanted to make it look like a robbery so as to obscure the real motive, the real *WHY*. "If they want you to be guilty, you're gonna be guilty, Joel. Irregardless."

"Why would they want me to be guilty?"

"Why? It's obvious."

"Let me get this straight: what you're saying, Fiedler, is that it doesn't matter if I'm innocent. It doesn't matter if I didn't kill Marsha and if her killer is out there killing other women."

"No, that's not what I'm saying."

"What are you saying?" I wonder briefly why I haven't fired this man. Truthfully, I don't think I know how to fire somebody. My mother once fired a cleaning lady who chatted on her cell phone and didn't clean. I would never have fired her. I would keep hoping that things would get better.

Fiedler continues. "It matters if the real criminal is still out there. It just doesn't matter to the police. Not after you confessed."

I stare at my lawyer, taking this in. He starts to number items on his left hand with his right index finger.

"For starters," he says, touching his left pinky, "they don't want to be bothered anymore. They have other cases to deal with. To them, number two," he taps his left ring finger, "the case is solved."

He then taps his left middle finger in much the same way that the bald waiter had tapped my menu in his palm. He is trying to remember number three. "Oh, yes, they don't want to be exposed. That they used coercive techniques to extract your confession, because you know, Joel, that would invalidate your confession. That's why we went after Fifth Amendment rights on appeal. At the hearing, the judge ruled that your confession was voluntary, and that was why she allowed it to be used at the trial. If the court overturned her ruling, the judge would look bad too."

Fiedler is making sense for a change.

"But your confession wasn't voluntary, right? At least you said it wasn't voluntary."

I suddenly feel dizzy. I'll fall over if I stand, just like I did at Marsha's bedside. "Do you doubt me, Fiedler?"

"No."

His 'no' inspires no confidence. "'At least you said it wasn't voluntary'. That sounds like doubt to me, Fiedler."

"That's lawyerly. I'm your lawyer, Joel. Lawyers must be careful. The point I'm making is that if we find the real killer, the confession will be seen as having been coerced. The cops don't want that."

I let this sink in, thinking again that the so-called officers of the court are engaged in a game with rules and language that outsiders cannot possibly understand. "Is there a number four?"

Fiedler looks puzzled, then remembers, because his right index finger is still touching his left middle finger. He moves to the left index finger. A key point must be coming.

"Yes. Number four. Yes. You reminded me. They believe you really are guilty. They've convinced themselves. It's called tunnel vision."

"They never even looked for anyone else."

"That's tunnel vision. No forced entry. Marriage squabbles. Baby on the way. It all added up…to them. They think they're smart, and they are, just not in the way we would like them to be. They're smart in making it look like you killed your wife. They're dumb when it comes to finding out who really did it. That begins number five."

He moves his index finger to the left thumb. "They don't want to look dumb. Try calling one of them a dumb cop." Fiedler stops and stares, shaking his head. "What were we talking about?"

"Why they need me to be guilty."

"Right."

"So that's why we need a dick."

"A what?"

"You know. A private eye."

Again, Fiedler stares blankly.

"We need a private eye to find Marsha's killer!"

"Yes, yes, you'll have to hire a private eye. I happen to know one. He's a former cop. D.D. O'Keefe. Former cops make the best private eyes. They know the ins and outs of the system."

"Do I have a choice?"

He shakes his head. "It's the only way we can solve the case."

"What I meant is, can I choose from a few of them?"

Fiedler shakes his head. "O'Keefe is the best in New York. He won't be out to rob you like most of them do."

"All right, I guess." I lack enthusiasm, thinking that Fielder is exaggerating in the manner of most New Yorkers, but I go along.

"He'll need a retainer."

"You mean like lawyers get?"

"Yes, a retainer. Five thousand or so I think he charges."

"I have to pay this guy five thousand dollars before he's done anything? You know, Fiedler, when people get in my cab, I don't ask for a retainer. I have to get them where they want to go and then they pay me. Why should I pay this guy before he gets me where I want to go?"

"I don't know. Maybe because he doesn't have a meter." Fiedler chuckles. We watch together as a cluster of roaches—their boldness continually amazes me—zero in on his briefcase. He picks it up and places it on the table. His lunch must be in there.

An abyss, a pit, a chasm opens up. It's ennui. It's atrophy. What the fuck? It's entropy. It's hopelessness but that's not all bad, because the pit of hopelessness is the safest place to be inside a prison. Hope, on the other hand, is dangerous, but hope is the only positive thing I have.

I want Fiedler to leave now. I have to go and do my prison job for which I get paid fourteen cents an hour. Money I use to dump into the food and drink machines at the end of every month, just like everyone else. I started out here working as a teacher. Me, a teacher! I am literate so they thought I could help other inmates get their GED's. After a week, I asked to mop and wax floors instead. The good thing about mopping and waxing floors is that it gives me the power to change something: keep the vermin at bay, make a dirty floor and a piss-filled common bathroom clean for a couple of hours. The mind and soul of a prisoner cannot be cleaned or polished by education, even temporarily, inside the walls of a prison.

"I'll bring along MacSweeney with O'Keefe next time."

"Wow."

"Joel, you gotta open doors, don't forget, byways, you don't leave stones unturned. You're not above anything when you're in here."

"Thanks for the reminder. Look, I have to go mop the floors. Come back soon, okay?"

We stand up and shake hands. He's right. Don't leave a stone unturned. My lawyer shuffles off to the free world.

With a snap of latex, Williams appears out of nowhere, like Jiminy Cricket or Mephistopheles. "Forgot to ask if you got the box, my man." Williams asks.

"Yeah. Thanks."

"I didn't do no C.O.D."

"Of course. How much did it come to?"

"Ninety-five. Minus the two flosses—compliments of the house—it comes to eighty-nine and change."

"That's more than you said."

"It's them drug companies. No keeping up with them multinationals."

"How much of the eighty-nine goes to your service charge?"

"Don't forget, them pharmacists charge dispensing fees."

We walk toward the sliding doors.

"Pharmacist says use it twice a day. Wash out the innie, dry it good, apply the oil and then the Lamisil. Says it may take a few weeks. And keep that innie dry, my man."

"Thanks."

"You need some Q-tips?"

"Yeah."

"That'll cost you." Williams snickers.

O

Exiting my own building with the police, I began to think of the many times as a cab driver I had witnessed the arrests of others. In every case, I equated the arrest with guilt and, despite whatever is said to the contrary about presumption of innocence and trial by jury, I know the cops do too. The impassive African American cop, who I hadn't noticed leaving the building with us, put his hand on top of my head as I got into the police car. I could have gotten into the car myself, but he seemed to think that I had to be squished in like a Jack-in-the-Box. This unnecessary cramming, this unfriendly hand on the head, gave me the feeling that I was being controlled and minimized. To make matters worse, my knees were squeezed up painfully against the front seat and the passenger windows were caged from the inside. Going over to the local precinct, the driver cop and Swain were silent. I certainly had nothing to say, although I wanted to tell the driver cop to slow down. I tried to review the morning's events, the record store, the coffee shop, the trip back on the subway, the walk through the subway tracks, the air-conditioned taxicab, the moment when I discovered Marsha, and the 911 call. An ordinary Sunday in which I was the sole agent of action had now turned into something in which I had no agency at all. *Calm down*, I told myself, *Be like those Brits you met on the boat while honeymooning with Marsha, calm in the face of roiling waters from an angry sea.* These weather-beaten men and women stood talking insouciantly about the places they had been to and where they were going next, while I excused myself to go vomit in the cabin. The English are people to emulate when you get into a tight spot and I was, to say the least, in a tight spot. I tried to reassure myself that as an innocent man I shouldn't be worried, but my mind was split in two. My wife was dead but, at the same time, I was being taken in for questioning. I could not feel the grief that I should have been feeling. Because grief and fear mix no better than oil and water, the fear separated and rose to the top.

The driver cop pulled into a space in front of the building. I wanted to open the door but looked in vain for a handle. Swain got out and opened the door for me. He put out a helping hand so that I could get out of the seat without twisting myself into a pretzel. "Come this way, Mr. Ascher. We have a few questions we want to ask you and then you can go on home. Just some details we'd like to clear up without people standing around. Okay?"

How could I refuse? I just followed and did what I was told. Somewhere in the back of my mind was a warning voice: *Name, address, and telephone number. Then ask to make a phone call.* But then I told myself that such precautions are for criminals and would be unnecessary for an innocent man. I wanted to talk to them. I wanted to tell them the truth as much as I believed they wanted to hear it.

The police station was not very busy. Except for the person who killed Marsha that morning, I guessed it was too hot for even criminals to be active. Some officers were standing around and chewing the fat. Chewing the fat. Shooting the shit. Prison language. I'm sounding more and more like a mug in a film noir, riding in a black sedan in the rain, listening to the purr of the engine and the comforting sound of the windshield wipers. I needed that comfort right then and there. They ushered me into a drab room with a desk, an old telephone, two chairs, and what was obviously a two-way mirror. I knew that I'd be speaking not just to Swain but to the observers behind the glass as well. It made me feel exposed, like an actor on opening night, but then I told myself that I didn't need to act at all.

I started thinking again that Marsha was dead and that her body was at the morgue. She was not at some funeral parlor. She was at a morgue where the coroner was probing her and cutting into the softness of her skin. My kind and beautiful wife, who I had kissed goodbye that morning on my way to find a rare Verdi recording, was having an autopsy, not a checkup or a cavity filled, but an autopsy. My wife, Marsha, had been murdered and I was sitting in an interrogation room talking to a detective with a very red face and very white hair, a head of granite with stark features that became more alarming with every minute. I was about to be questioned regarding the murder; I knew that. But first, my interrogator excused himself to leave the room.

"You don't mind but I gotta take a whiz."

This man who I feared had just said the most casual thing, words you might use when addressing a buddy in a bar. "I gotta take a whiz," is what he said.

I was encouraged to engage in the same informality. "I'd also like to…take a whiz…if you don't mind."

Captain Swain stared at me as if I was being flippant. I mean he was allowed to take a whiz but a man whose wife had just been murdered was not allowed to take a whiz, much less even *say* take a whiz. Then I thought that he really didn't have to take a whiz; what he wanted to do was make me want to take a whiz. All he needed to do next was turn on a faucet and the torture would be acute. That thought, that sudden conviction that he was messing with my head, confirmed to me that I really was a suspect. Otherwise, why wouldn't he just allow me to piss? In turn, knowing that I was a suspect made me nervous, making me want to piss even more.

The captain left the room and I was left waiting. I also recognized this as a tactic. Staring at the two-way mirror, I clasped my hands on the back of my head and just stared back. Of course Swain, unless he really had gone to take a whiz, was staring from behind the mirror as well. After a short while, he came back in and reintroduced himself.

"Police Captain Hal Swain," he said, as he held out his hand to shake mine. Very friendly he was. "As I said, Mr. Ascher, I think I'll call you Joel, if you don't mind, I have a few questions to ask you and then we'll take you home. You must be distraught."

"Yes, I am distraught. Of course I'm distraught. My wife is dead and I'm not going to have a baby." Swain laughed. I could not believe how stupid I sounded.

"Did you cut yourself?"

"No, why do you ask?"

"Your hand."

I looked and saw that the outside of my hand was stained with Marsha's blood. I had forgotten. How is it I had forgotten?

"That's my wife's blood. I put my hand on the sheet when I turned her over."

"Mmm hmm. And what's that?" He pointed to a smear of blood I had also failed to notice on the right side of my checked short-sleeved shirt. That's your wife's blood too. No?"

"Yes, of course. I must have gotten that from the bed sheet as well."

"You got it from the bed sheet?"

"Yes. Now look, Mr. Swain, Captain Swain, Sir, I hope you're not even suggesting that I killed my own wife."

"Who suggested anything?"

"I think I better call a lawyer. Yes, I want to call a lawyer."

"You have something to hide, Joel?"

"I have nothing to hide but I don't like the tenor of your questioning."

"There's nothing official here. I haven't even read you your Miranda rights. I'm just trying to clear up some details. But I tell you what, Joel. I'll read you your rights and then you can decide whether you want to talk to me or to a lawyer. Of course, if you ask for a lawyer, you'll be sitting here for some time. Don't forget that it's Sunday. Your lawyer is liable to be on the golf course or maybe at the beach."

I certainly did not like his tone. "I don't have a lawyer and I don't know any lawyers."

"That's too bad, Joel. It's always wise to have a lawyer at the ready—just in case. Someone to be in your corner."

"Do you know any lawyers?"

"We're not supposed to recommend lawyers, Joel. Not usually."

"I can understand that, Hal…Captain Swain. Still, maybe you can make an exception this time?"

"Well, Joel, I do happen to know someone who's pretty reliable. But I can't take responsibility for that."

"What's his name?"

"He might even be free to help you today. He's like a doctor on call, except that he's a lawyer."

God, did I ever have to piss! "Wait a minute, Swain, why do I need a lawyer? How did we get to this? I thought this was going to be a conversation. I thought you wanted me to clear up a few details. Isn't that what you said?"

"Yes, that's what I said. But a few surprising things have come up here, you know, blood stains and all the rest, so I'm going to have to read you your rights."

"I'm not under arrest, am I?"

"Not exactly, Joel."

"Exactly? Exactly what is my status?"

"You're under investigation. You're a possible suspect in the murder of your wife. Don't look surprised. Most murders occur during domestic disputes. We first need to dispose of you as a suspect so we can go after the person who actually killed her."

"If I'm not under arrest, if I'm only a suspect, then I'm free to leave. Right?"

"Yes, that's right. If you choose to leave, we'll conduct our investigation without your input. And, of course, we'll draw our own conclusions."

What he said seemed very reasonable. I hadn't done anything wrong so why not just cooperate and get it over with?

"If I read you your rights, it's only a precaution that helps you. It helps you to think about what you're saying."

I was confused, definitely confused. I didn't want to appear guilty by avoiding Swain's questions but I couldn't understand why I needed to be interrogated—this was an interrogation room, after all. Reluctantly, I nodded, thinking of those intrepid Brits on the boat. I could get through this, I told myself, but I had to be on my guard.

"Anything you say to me may be held against you in a court of law. You are free, without prejudicing your rights, not to answer any of my questions. Do you understand?"

"Yes." That qualifier, the right not to answer particular questions, seemed liberal to me.

"And you can decide at any time to stop answering my questions if you need to speak to a lawyer. Do you understand?"

I nodded. It all sounded good. He gave me a document, a waiver, he called it, that said I was agreeing to questioning without a lawyer being present. I signed it.

"Would you like to make a phone call?"

It so much sounded like I was under arrest.

"Maybe so. Maybe I should have a lawyer."

"All right. I assume you can afford to pay for counsel." Swain sounded so flexible and accommodating. I'd signed the waiver but I could see he wasn't going to take advantage.

"Yes, I can afford counsel. What about the lawyer you mentioned? The one who'll come right over?"

Swain smiled. "You mean Syd, Syd Fiedler? I'm sure that you two will get along like gangbusters."

"'Gangbusters'. Yes, I suppose."

"You two speak the same language—so to speak." Swain stood, reached into his back pocket for his wallet and pulled out a business card. "Here's the phone number." He pointed to the phone and then excused himself.

"Captain Swain?"

"Yes?"

"I really need to pee. Really bad." I thought that *pee* was the proper word under the circumstances. *Piss* was too macho and I didn't want to present myself that way. To say 'take a whiz' again would sound like mockery. And *use the washroom* sounded timid.

"Sure thing, Joel. Out in the hallway, turn right; it's the third door on your left. First just give me your shirt. I want to run it upstairs for testing." Tearing open a Handi Wipe that he'd taken from his pocket, he picked up my bloodied right hand, "Let me do a little dab on that."

I gave him my shirt and ran topless to the men's room. First, I did my business. Oh, such relief! Then, seeing a horror movie character, a regular Dracula in the mirror, I washed my hands and face, splashed soap and water under my arms, and used several brown paper towels to dry off. When I returned, Fiedler's card was still sitting next to the telephone. Why didn't I just get up and leave? It would look bad and they'd investigate without my input; that's what Swain had said. And I certainly didn't want to appear ungrateful. So I punched in the number. A recording came on.

"Not to worry. You've reached Sydney Fiedler, attorney-at-law in the great city of New York. At the beep, please leave your name, number, the time of your call and your present situation, and I'll return your call as soon as possible."

"Joel Ascher..." There was no number printed on the phone. "I'm at a precinct, I think maybe the 34th Precinct in Manhattan, and Captain Swain, Hal Swain, told me to call you. I'm being investigated for my wife's murder...which I didn't do." I hung up, thinking that the people looking on from behind the mirror might have been impressed by my calm and my claim of innocence.

After I had waited topless and played with my nipples for what seemed to be an hour, Swain came back into the room. "So, Joel, is Fiedler on his way?"

"I asked him to call the precinct."

"Then he should get back to you sooner or later. They'll patch it in here. You'll excuse me, Joel, but I have some other business to attend to."

"What about getting me a shirt, Captain?"

"Of course, Joel. Soon." Out he went.

So I sat there waiting, still topless, for Fiedler to call. Maybe this lawyer was dealing with another case in another precinct? Maybe *he* was on the golf course or at the beach? I got to my feet, stared into the mirror and went to the door of the interrogation room. I opened it again and stared out into the hallway. A heavily made up female cop with blond hair tucked beneath her cap, happened to walk by.

"Excuse me?" I ventured.

She stopped and looked but didn't respond. She stared at me as if I had some communicable disease.

"Do you have any magazines around here? Something I can read? Even police magazines. What about police manuals? Maybe police procedure manuals? That might be interesting. Maybe you have some legal books lying around? I'd like to read about the law. No? What about journals? Do you have any law journals?"

With every question I asked, she seemed more and more puzzled, as if I'd been speaking in tongues. She walked away without answering. I went back inside the room to sit.

Dispiriting hours passed in contemplation of my unattractive body and my situation, hours broken only by the driver cop coming in with a cup of water or *Nuts and Bolts*, even a small package of cookies. I would doze off for a short time but would be interrupted by the driver cop. He appeared to be playing the role of a flight attendant. One time he came in with magazines, although I would have preferred a shirt, reminding me that I'd asked Laura, whom I assumed was the made up cop with the blond hair, to provide some reading material. He presented me with three old *Reader's Digests* and a *Better Homes and Gardens*. I began a *Reader's Digest* from July 1994. For some reason, maybe a very good reason, I remember the date but not the article I read. Finally, I got up to leave. I wasn't under arrest after all. Swain told me that I wasn't under arrest. Or did he? What difference did it make? They could always come and get me when they wanted to. Who cared what they thought about me anyway? Let them conduct their own investigation without my input if they wanted. I looked into the mirror and gave a little wave. Yes, I would leave, even if I were half naked. I walked out into the hall and froze in place; I wanted to leave but was overcome by fear. I came back inside and sat down again. I stared at the phone and began nodding off. When it rang, I jumped, just as if someone had fired off a gun in the room. I picked up the receiver.

"Yes?"

"Joel Ascher? Is this Joel? You called. It's Sydney, Sydney Fiedler."

I wanted to weep. "Sydney."

"You're in trouble, Joel?"

"Yes." He sounded so solicitous that I almost started crying. "I mean no. I haven't done anything but they have me here for questioning. Can you come down?"

"I'm in Yonkers. My sister is ill. I can be there tomorrow though."

"Should I leave?"

"No. You shouldn't do that. Unless you got something to hide, just answer their questions." This seemed a little strange to me but who was I to argue with a lawyer? "Did they read you your rights?"

"Yes."

"That's good. That's very good, Joel. Now you're protected."

"I'm protected? I think they're protected. Do you mind telling me what kind of lawyer you are?"

"A criminal defense attorney. Stay calm, Joel. Don't answer *all* the questions. Just answer the questions you want to answer, and then they'll let you go home. You said that your wife's been killed. I'm so sorry to hear that. You must have business to attend to."

"Yes, I do." Although what business it was I couldn't begin to contemplate. "Are you sure you can't come now?"

"I can't until tomorrow. I'll meet you there tomorrow morning. If necessary, I'll come down to meet you. Maybe it won't be necessary and you can save some money."

From what I knew of lawyers, that was also an unusual thing to say. Had I stereotyped the whole profession? I hung up and continued to wait. Then I tried to call my parents. Not that

I wanted to call them because I knew they would lose it. I mean how could I minimize Marsha's murder and me being a suspect? But I needed to speak to someone I knew. If they weren't home, I'd try my brother, Ed. As soon as my parents' phone rang, the driver cop came into the room. At last! I hung up the receiver just as my mother said "Hello."

"Captain Swain said to tell you that he's on his way up. Sit tight."

I waited another ten minutes and tried to call my parents again. The extension had gone dead so I couldn't dial out. It had to be late, so I thought that the operator had gone home.

Finally, Swain appeared again with a tray holding a pitcher of water and a glass. I could have hugged him.

"Did Fiedler call?"

I downed two glasses of water and thought the better of a third since I didn't want to have to pee again. "As a matter of fact, he did. And he told me to answer your questions so I could go home."

"He's not coming?"

"He's in Yonkers with his sick sister. He'll be here tomorrow if I need him."

"Truthfully, I don't think you'll need him. Do you?"

"No, I think you're right."

"He's a crack lawyer, though. Very sharp."

"I'm sure he is. He sounded very kind too."

"Yes, he is. I can assure you. Are we all right now? Good. Let's get started, Joel. Let's get you on your way. Just tell me about this morning."

So I went through the story from the kiss goodbye to the discovery of the body. At every juncture he asked a question. If he'd go back to something I had already answered, my follow-up answers were fairly consistent—at least I think they were. Somewhere inside me I knew I was making a mistake by talking to him, but I didn't listen to my inner voice.

Then they changed cops on me. Of course they changed cops. Anyone who watches TV crime shows and crime movies knows that they change cops. Captain Swain was Mr. Nice Guy and Detective Irving, a fireplug with an anchor tattooed on his right forearm, was Mr. Hard Guy. Detective Irving was accompanied by Detective Paulie. Or was it Polly? She wasn't too nice either. I'm sure that Irving and Paulie must have been observing me through the two-way mirror. She took notes but occasionally chimed in with an edgy question, even a nasty question. I was tired, dog-tired and still half-naked. I just wanted the whole thing to end; I wanted the whole terrible day to go away.

"You're telling us that you rolled your wife's body over and saw the knife sticking out of her chest?" asked Detective Irving, in a doubtful way.

"That's what I told you. That's what I'm telling you."

"You expect us to believe bullshit like that?" I was surprised to hear Sergeant Paulie say that.

"You had blood on your hands," Irving continued. He appeared to be on the verge of throwing a punch.

"More like he *has* blood on his hands," Paulie added.

"And on your clothes!" Suddenly, Irving's fist jerked forward and I started back. He stopped mid-punch, and rubbed the bridge of his nose instead. From that point on, he made a fist every time he moved his arm, causing me to flinch.

"Are you some kind of psycho, Joel?" Paulie was poised to write the answer on her pad.

"No." What answer did she expect?

"Then stop with the bullshit." I must have looked uncomprehending. "That bullshit about going down to the Village. You're not gay, are you?" Irving laughed at his colleague's suggestion.

The two homophobes peppered me like that for an hour or two or three. Limiting themselves to crude personal attacks, not once did they ask me if I had killed Marsha. By the time Swain returned, looking refreshed, I was sure it was tomorrow. It was a new day but this ugly thing was not about to go away.

"He's all yours," said Irving. Both homophobes gave me contemptuous looks and left the room.

"Look, Swain, I'm tired and I need to sleep. I'll come back tomorrow with…with my lawyer."

"We're just about done, Joel. We'll give you a ride home."

I was thankful for his consideration but I sighed. The sigh was a tacit agreement that I'd go on for ten more minutes at the most. I was getting a ride, after all.

"Joel, all of us here have troubles at home. We know what it's like to feel annoyed with our spouses. Sometimes things build up. We know that. Sometimes we strike out and hurt each other."

"No, no, no, no, Detective. I did not strike out like that. I'm a non-violent person."

"I tell you what, Joel, just to sum things up, why don't we go through your day in reverse. Start with coming here and work your way back to getting out of bed this morning. Then off we go. Okay?"

I didn't even have the energy to nod. I was feeling as if I'd been run over. So I began by entering the police station and working my way back through the discovery of Marsha's killing, the cab ride, the walk through the subway tunnel, the coffee, the record store, the subway down and the kiss goodbye to Marsha. Marsha was already beginning to feel irrelevant to the story and the details began to seem fabricated. Plus I hadn't felt boredom like this since high school math.

"Joel, my friend, you did a great job there going in reverse. Thank you." I was extremely pleased with myself and started to get up. "Still…it seems a little too well rehearsed." He might have stuck the sharpened tip of a poisoned umbrella into me and I would have felt less pain. "Now, suppose you tell me why you went off this morning, your day off, and spent it by yourself down in the Village…and not with your wife? What else did you do down there?"

I fell back into my chair. "I always do the same thing. I have a cappuccino and read *The Times*." I suddenly remembered that

I was forced, despite my protests, to leave the paper behind me when we evacuated the subway.

"Didn't you think she'd enjoy that? Having cappuccino with you?"

"Maybe. But she's busy right now studying for her law exams."

"You mean she *was* busy studying."

"Yes, she was. She was." It was a low blow. Did he expect me to have gotten used to her being gone forever? "Now, look, today is not really my day off. Saturday afternoon begins my day off. I don't work Saturday nights. I work tonight. So I have Sunday morning to myself." I hardly knew what I was blathering on about and Swain didn't much care.

"What café were you at?"

I couldn't remember; the Village is one big café.

"Your relationship wasn't very good, was it?"

"Who told you that? It's not true."

"What did you do between waking up and leaving your house? Before this kiss goodbye?"

"Are you sure this is the end, Swain?"

"I promise. You got my word of honor, Joel." By then, his childish promise sounded ominous.

"Okay. I got up. I turned on the coffee machine. I...I uh, shaved." I felt my face. Maybe I hadn't shaved. The way Swain stared made me think he'd caught me in a lie. "I took a shower. I...I had some granola and yogurt...with fruit."

"You cut up the fruit?"

"Of course."

"With the same knife you said you found in Marsha's chest?"

"That's the truth."

"What else did you do?"

I started to rush just to get the questioning over with. "I drank some coffee with half and half. Oh, I also had half of a prune Danish. I left the dishes in the sink—"

The faster I spoke, the slower he asked his questions. "Do you always do that? Leave your dirty dishes in the sink?"

"No, I didn't want to wake her up."

"Who? Who didn't you want to wake up?"

I stared at Swain, thinking that he was either stupid or as bored as I was.

"You don't like saying her name, do you, Joel?"

"Marsha? Who else would it be? I assumed you knew we lived together."

"Yes."

"What else do you want to know? I brushed my teeth and left."

"Joel, before you claimed to have left the apartment and returned home, Marsha was murdered. The coroner phoned in just a short time ago to say she was murdered around 9 a.m."

"How do they know the time she was murdered?"

"These days they know everything. They can tell by the contents of the stomach, the coagulation of the blood, the presence of adrenaline in the bloodstream. Lots of ways."

"She was not dead when I left." He was lying to me; I was sure of that.

"Yes, she was."

"I want a lawyer and I want to go home." I was beginning to sound like a child.

"Sure you do, Joel. But you won't be leaving here just yet."

"I told you I have to go to work tonight."

"You're going to work tonight? Your wife was murdered today."

"Of course, I'm sorry." I was appalled at myself. My mind had stopped working; more and worse blunders were to come.

"I can understand, Joel. We're all creatures of habit. What I was saying before, Joel, is that we all have feelings of wanting to strike out, but we don't always act on them. Some of us have stronger feelings than others and we're not aware of the strength of those feelings."

"All right, what are you getting at, Swain?" I wanted to say 'swine' but I didn't. That showed me I still had self-control.

"Maybe you didn't kill Marsha, not consciously. I believe you when you say you didn't do it. Maybe you…you blacked out and something inside you, some other Joel, killed her under compulsion. Unconsciously. Maybe this Joel walked into the kitchen, cut up his fruit, wiped off the knife and blacked out. He didn't know what he was doing, right? He took the knife and plunged it into Marsha's chest. This angry Joel. Right?"

"What the fuck are you talking about?"

"I'm talking about what you don't remember."

"How am I supposed to know what I can't remember?"

"I'm helping you do that, Joel."

"This is sick, Swain." I was sweating badly, and with no shirt to absorb it, a stain was spreading on my pants, reminding me of my worst elementary school humiliation.

"Shall I give you some time to think it over? You know if that's what happened, the worst you get is involuntary manslaughter."

"I'm telling you this is bullshit." I was so tired, that my voice was no longer attached to my will.

"Are you telling me, Joel, that it was impossible that you blacked out and killed Marsha?"

"Bullshit, Swain. You're a cocksucker!" I heard my voice say that. I couldn't believe I had just called a police captain a cocksucker. Calling him a cocksucker was way worse than calling him dumb. All I wanted at that moment was sleep.

"Impossible? Impossible? Impossible, Joel, that you might do something you couldn't control and then regret it?" His voice was insinuating, like a hypnotist.

"Maybe not impossible. But the fact remains that I did not kill my wife."

"So it was possible?"

"No, that's different."

"Possible is the opposite of impossible. By definition, Joel."

"The fact remains—"

"The fact is, Joel, that what you think of as fact may not be fact at all."

My forehead fell into my hand. My eyes closed. I started to sleep in that position.

Swain's voice intruded. "Was it *possible* that you lost control and blacked out? That you did something you wouldn't normally do? Just like you did now when you called me a cocksucker?"

"All right, already, it was possible! Anything is possible. Maybe you're a gremlin. Now shut the fuck up and let me go to sleep."

"So you say it was possible that you killed Marsha?"

I looked up at him. "Sure. I told you. And who knows who else I killed?"

Swain smiled and turned slowly to the two-way mirror. "Did you get that?"

After a moment, Irving and Paulie came scurrying back into the room. "That qualifies, don't you think?" Swain asked.

"It certainly qualifies," said Paulie. "It qualified in *Tankleff vs. The State of New York* and it'll qualify here."

Swain put a hand on my shoulder and said, "Thank you, Joel. You did really well. I know how rough this kind of thing can be. But now it's all out in the open. All you need to do is say it on camera and you may even be able to plead temporary insanity."

He sounded so comforting. The driver cop came in with a towel to wipe myself with and a coarse t-shirt, both smelling of some repulsive floral detergent. They went out. I sat in the interrogation room and waited again, nodding off and awakening time after time.

Finally, they came back and led me into a room with a video camera. I don't remember seeing a cameraman but one must have been there. I've seen the video, seen myself talking to Swain, seen myself repeating what I'd told him about how I may have blacked out. I was in a trance. To have repeated those words on camera was the true temporary insanity.

So you say it was possible that you killed Marsha?

Sure. I told you. And who knows who else I killed?

At the end of the filming, Swain said to Irving, "I want you to take Joel downstairs, give him something to eat and drink, something more to wear and find him a bed. He needs some sleep."

Swain's suggestion that Irving find me a bed startled me. I held out a hand, gesturing to Irving to stop.

"I'd rather sleep at home, Swain…that is, if you don't mind."

"Well, the thing is, Joel, we kind of want you to sleep here."

"Just call me a cab, okay. I'll be back tomorrow."

"But you might oversleep and then you would miss your arraignment."

"Don't worry, I won't—" It hit me then. Tired as I was, the conclusion was now inescapable. "I'm under arrest, aren't I?"

Irving and Paulie started laughing together. "Bingo!"

Swain said to them blandly, "It's not funny. This is no laughing matter." To me he said, "By the time you wake up, Joel, your lawyer should be here."

"My lawyer? The Sydney guy?"

The mood had changed, the tension lifted. I knew something had happened but the consequences meant nothing to me. Only sleep meant anything. I could eat sleep; I could drown in sleep.

"I think I'll go down with you guys," Swain told them. I remember showering but I don't remember anything after that until Swain dropped me at an empty cell. They had given me some other clothes to wear, boxer shorts, a drab green shirt and pants smelling of the same floral detergent. Swain directed me through an open cell door. "Here you go, Joel. It's private." The cell was every bit a cell. A metal toilet and, attached to the wall, a fold down bed upon which was something that might be termed a mattress if you happened to be a bedbug.

Just before he left, Swain told me to give my shoelaces to Detective Irving. I wondered about this at the time although I understand perfectly now.

I had stopped talking by then. I should have stopped sooner. But, I thought to myself, *A private cell. Maybe that's a good sign.*

Paulie locked the door. "Get a good rest, Joel. We'll see you in the morning."

"What morning? What day is it?"

"Monday night, my friend," said Swain.

Even on that bed, I slept.

O

I am now on the main floor with my faded lawyer. A blizzard of snowflakes has piled up on his shoulders. He has grabbed hold of my elbow to steady me. We are once again in a brightly lit hotel corridor, walking on low pile carpet, not actually walking now but trudging as if on a forced march. We pass a buzzing ice machine and reach doorway number 163. My faded lawyer looks up at me with a look that says, *Are you sure you want to go through with this?* A world with limited speech becomes a series of gestures, and we can say so much without speaking a word. I have come to appreciate the work of my faded lawyer, a man of few words.

I nod. I will go into this room, room number 163. My lawyer puts his right arm around my shoulders. With his left hand he slides in the key card and pulls it out. Once again, the light turns green. He pulls down the handle and pushes open the door. On the bed is a form, a nude body lying on its side with its back to me, showing a fine curvature of the hip. I hesitate. My lawyer nudges me forward; he stays outside as the door closes. I walk to the bed, my spirits lifting. Suddenly I am ecstatic. I am almost floating, so light I want to laugh. And then I am laughing. I approach and stand over her, placing a hand on her soft shoulder. She turns to face me. Her red hair undone, she stares at me from her full round face, mouth accentuated by Cupid's bow. She is no dream vision either; she is real. I am certain that she is real, more real than she's ever been. She is Marsha and not Marsha. She is the face beneath the face.

I speak silently. "Marsha."

Her stare is alert but her lips do not move.

I am unable to read her. Why can I understand my faded lawyer and not my own wife? But then I think I understand; yes, I think I understand. She is staring at me, not at my flesh, not at my face, but at me, the me that lies beneath my face. Both of us are naked before each other for the first time.

I start to speak. She smiles.

The bed shakes. In desperation, I shut my eyes and try to claw my way back into the dream. I can no more do that than return from the dead. "Jesus, what are you doing down there?" I ask Hernandez. I have never been so disgusted to see another human being or, to be exact, the plumber's crack of another human being.

"I wake you up. I am sorry, Huel. I need to borrow the foongus stuff. My *cojones* I think has the foongus."

"It's in the goddamn shoebox. A white tube."

"Thank you, Huel." He pulls out the shoebox and takes out the tube. "What's it say here, Huel?"

"Two times daily."

"Two times? When?"

"Morning and evening. Fuck knows."

"Sorry I wake you, Huel."

"You should be sorry."

"*Gracias*. Thank you for this."

"Don't mention it. Please don't mention it."

Our cell door slides open. It's dinnertime. Prisoners walk by swearing and laughing. Why does my body keep demanding food? First we eat what they call dinner and then we watch television. What sport will they have on? What team will they be rooting for? Sad, when I think about it, that most people live this way, some of them free to do whatever they please. Am I any different?

Victor squeezes a major dollop of Lamisil into his palm. "You should wash it out first, Hernandez. Use the tea tree oil. It won't do you any good otherwise. And you only need to use a little bit."

"I think I need a lot. Thank you, Huel." He lathers it under his balls.

Jesus. Jesus. Jesus.

O

"D.D. O'Keefe." The stocky P.I., that's what they call a dick now, a P.I. for private investigator, holds out his powerful meaty hand and crushes mine. MacSweeney is not with him.

"D.D.?"

"Right, Dennis Devlin O'Keefe."

"He's going to solve the case, Joel." Fiedler is smiling hard, as if he's won the lottery.

"It's taken you guys a while. Ed paid you the retainer over a month ago."

"D.D. is a busy man, Joel. He's out solving cases all over New York."

"It's a trip up here, Joel. You need to pack a lunch."

"Well, I'm glad you made it, finally."

"It's not as if I haven't been working on your case. I read the trial transcripts and narrowed down the witnesses that Fiedler and I need to visit. I combed the police reports and found a few inconsistencies." He pulls out a sheaf of papers from a leather briefcase. I start to feel hope as we pore over these documents.

O'Keefe pauses over a page of trial transcript. "I think you got a good case here for ineffective assistance of counsel."

Fiedler's mouth drops. O'Keefe is not making an attempt at humor but he breaks into forced laughter. "Just kidding, Sydney."

To me, he says, "Lousy weather out there."

"Inside here it's either too hot or too cold," I say.

"He was just joking, Joel. That's what D.D. is like. He's a very ironic man."

"I'm glad to hear that, D.D., about the irony. We should get along. So where are we at?"

O'Keefe resumes his confident tone, using words that he must have learned at a weekend workshop for P.I.'s. "We're preparing to hit the road. When the journey is over, you're going to know who killed your wife and then you'll walk out of here a free man."

"You really think so?" O'Keefe's confidence has caught me in its wake.

Fiedler puts a hand on my arm. "He's the best, Joel." O'Keefe sits back and smiles. "If anyone can set you free, it's going to be D.D."

"That has a ring to it. You should put Fiedler's recommendation in an advertisement, D.D."

"That *is* my advertisement." O'Keefe pulls out his business card and hands it to me. The phrase runs right through the center. I want to believe it. I really want to believe it.

O'Keefe gets down to business. "I need to know some things from you."

"Sure."

"First, I need to know if Marsha had enemies."

"Not that I know of. Even my parents loved her."

"She didn't owe something maybe? Maybe she was gambling behind your back?"

"I would have seen that in my bank account."

"Not necessarily. Do you know if she had her own account?"

"She did, but it was pin money. We looked at that, didn't we, Fiedler?"

"I can't remember."

"Then we'll take another look, Joel. Did Marsha belong to any groups? Maybe a pro-abortion group or something like that?"

"No group, no, but she *was* pro-choice."

"Hmm. Did she attend rallies?"

I'm impressed by his thoroughness. An ember of confidence begins to glow inside my chest. "Yes. Yes, she did. Do you think that may be it?"

"Probably not. They usually shoot their enemies. How about other men? Was she having an affair?" This is obviously the key question, the one he set me up for with the other bullshit.

"How should I know?"

"Most men know when their wives are having an affair. People in your generation usually tell each other."

"I don't think she was having an affair. She certainly didn't tell me." I'm not nearly as confident as I think I sound.

"That's good. Wouldn't you say that's good, Fiedler?" Fiedler nods. I have no idea what O'Keefe means by *good* and I'm not sure if Fiedler does either. "What about you, Joel?"

"An affair? I was not having an affair."

"Did you have enemies?"

"A lot of them. I've offended a lot of people."

"Who? Give me some names." O'Keefe pulls a pen from his pocket and a writing pad. To Fiedler, he says, "Now we're on to something. Didn't you ask him this before the trial?" O'Keefe stares at me. "Well, who did you offend?"

"Mrs. Grasso, my grade four teacher; Mr. Busk, my grade eight math teacher; Ms. Higgins, my high school principal... Oh, yeah, James Levine."

"Who is James Levine?" O'Keefe writes the name down.

"Never mind. I'm only kidding."

Fiedler jumps in. "D.D.'s time is valuable."

"I'm looking for a lead, Joel."

"I can't help you, D.D. I wish I knew why someone wanted to kill my wife. That's what I'm paying *you* for."

"Joel!" Fiedler cautions.

"Take some time, Joel, and get back to Fiedler." O'Keefe stands up abruptly, obviously miffed. "My clients always know more than they think."

"We'll be back soon, Joel," says Fiedler.

Williams approaches. Addressing Fiedler and O'Keefe, he says, "I'm hoping you guys get my brother out. I know the man is innocent. Wouldn't hurt a fly."

O'Keefe nods. "Don't worry. We will."

"You're in good hands," says Fiedler, standing as well.

"That also has a ring to it," I say, standing up to shake O'Keefe's hand.

"You're an ironic man too, Joel."

"I'm sorry. No offense intended. Hey, Fiedler, do you think you can do me a favor for your next visit? Can you bring Ed with you? There's just no damn way he'll come to this place by bus."

"Why should he take a bus?"

"He won't. That's why I'm asking you to bring him up here."

"Your brother doesn't need to take a bus and he doesn't need a ride from me. Your brother has a new car."

Suddenly I'm short of breath. As Fiedler and O'Keefe head for the free world, Williams and I walk toward the sliding door, passing underneath a pair of cameras mounted on opposite walls. I have an almost irresistible urge to flip the bird.

"You feelin' okay, my man?" Williams puts an arm around my shoulder. Any sign of friendship between a guard and a prisoner is not looked upon with favor by the watchers. I stare at him doubtfully. When he sees that I'm not going to collapse on to the floor, he removes his arm. "You ain't getting sick?"

I shake my head.

"Ascher, man, how can you keep a lawyer like that?"

"Fiedler, you mean?"

"That's who I mean."

"What do you know about lawyers, Williams?"

"What do I know 'bout lawyers? Listen to the man. What do I know 'bout lawyers? What do Einstein know 'bout atoms? Ain't a lawyer come in here don't slip me a card. I'm telling you I wouldn't trust that Fiedler, man. Fiedler some little snake in the grass."

The door slides open. "Don't worry, Williams, I won't be asking you to provide me with a lawyer."

"Just the same, my man."

The door behind us grinds slowly shut.

Williams shines the light into my mouth. "That floss is doin' the job, my man. How's that fungus doin'?"

"I gave the Lamisil and the tea tree oil to Hernandez."

"No shit?"

"I don't care if the fungus eats me alive."

Williams looks around then speaks softly. "Bend over, my man." He gestures toward the glass booth with his head, "You know them watchers is watching."

O

The morning of my arraignment kicked off another terrible day. I was still in a dream state from the interrogation when I was ushered into an almost empty courtroom by a burly guard. Burly, a word that sounds just like what it means. Fiedler met me at the defendant's table. He introduced himself for the first time and we shook hands.

As we sat down, he got right to business. "They'll be charging you with murder in the first degree."

"What's that word when something sounds the same as what it means?"

"The judge will ask you to plead guilty or not guilty." What had he just told me?

"Joel, how do you want to plead?"

"What are you talking about, Fiedler?" He stared at me as if I were some creature from an adjoining galaxy, just arrived on a flying saucer.

"You are being charged with first-degree murder. How do you want to plead?"

"Murder? Did you say first-degree murder? Are you crazy?" Maybe *he* had arrived on a flying saucer—from Yonkers.

"Murder one."

"They told me involuntary manslaughter at the worst. How can they lie like that?"

"They can lie all they like."

"Isn't that perjury, Fiedler?"

"They can't lie in court. That's perjury. But they can lie during interrogation."

"Who makes up these rules?" I was about to implode like a death star. There was no one and nothing I could trust.

"I told you not to answer all their questions."

"Why couldn't you come in like I asked you? I needed you to be there."

"My brother was sick. In Yonkers."

"Your brother? Your brother was sick? I thought you said your sister was sick?"

"Did I? I must have been upset. I meant brother. My brother Marcy has a bleeding ulcer."

"Sorry to hear it." I slowly shook my head. I saw more stragglers filing into the courtroom.

"Joel, they offered you a plea bargain already. They want to save the expense of a trial. If you plead guilty, they'll give you a shot at parole in fifteen years."

"Fifteen years! That's a bargain? I'm innocent!"

"I worked a good deal for you with the D.A.'s office. Fifteen to life. You won't even be fifty-five when you get out. Of course that's if you get parole."

"If I get parole?"

"Well, you should. But I can't guarantee it."

"Did you hear me? I…am…innocent! Innocent!" A small knot of people were now seated on the courtroom benches. All of them must have heard my outburst.

"So you won't be taking the plea?"

"All rise!" The clerk's voice was louder than mine, so loud that I almost fell over while jumping out of my chair. The tiny judge with the Jackie Kennedy bouffant walked in and sat way above us, with only her face visible. "This court is now in session, Judge Poliakoff presiding!"

A flock of lawyers gathered around the judge: the prosecutor, Alpha/Brookes and his assistants, along with Fiedler. They spoke amongst themselves while I sat there with the blood rushing through my ears. I heard nothing. I began to listen when the clerk read out the charge. Just as Fiedler had said, they were charging me with murder in the first degree for killing Marsha.

"How do you plead, Mr. Ascher?"

"Can I consult my lawyer, Judge—Your Honor?"

"Mr. Fiedler, have you not consulted with your client?"

"Of course I have, Your Honor." Fiedler leaned toward me. He spoke in a whisper. "How do you want to plead, Joel?"

I whispered back. "Tell me what to do."

"You say you're innocent. Plead not guilty, of course."

I stood up. "Not guilty…Your Honor." I had seen people do this in the movies more times than I could remember, but movies are a poor guide for how to behave in reality. I understood then what it meant to be an illiterate person, an alien in a world I knew nothing about, a world that spoke a language I could not understand.

O

The prison yard is a dusty rectangular expanse. No grass grows in this yard, no trees, just the cruel sun in the summer and sometimes the mercy of the clouds. Above the thirty-six foot high walls is razor wire, a shiny roll that is painful even to look at. There is a difference between wanting to die and actively pursuing it. Out in the yard, however, I don't need to impale myself on razor wire if I want to die.

Today, as usual, the yard was full of clusters of people, some playing games, some discussing the Bible with one of God's emissaries, other groups talking together about nothing, along with the loners like me. Most of the loners are mental patients on some kind of drug regimen, walking like zombies with anesthetized looks on their faces. A few are just on drugs, period. Three burly guards with clubs and walkie-talkies attached to their belts stood together chewing the fat, or their cud is really what it looked like. A baseball game was taking place at the far end on an improvised field. The bases were green prison-issue shirts, easily shed in the intense heat. At the near end, inmates competed furiously on a pocked asphalt basketball court. Basketball here is less a game than a life and death struggle for supremacy. The shouting is constant. Near the entrance to the yard, behind a set of high revolving doors, the kind with silver bars at the subway exits, shirtless men were pressing weights on a bench. A domino game was taking place in a small bit of shade cast by a guard tower. The shouts of the baseball and basketball games, the grunts of the weight lifters, the clacking of the dominoes made it seem as loud outside as it is indoors.

Seeing me, one of the basketball players, a tough little white hoodlum named Pierce, broke off and asked another guy to take his place. Entering the yard from the revolving gates was a guy called Nando. My stomach churned. There's no escaping this kind of thing. It's not as if I could walk across the street and catch a bus.

"Ascher, baby, did you get any of them chocolate chips again from your bro?" Pierce has adopted the language and hip-hop gestures, especially touching his genitals, of African Americans. Sharing booty, of course, is required. Prison is both a capitalist's dream and a socialist's paradise.

"How about my jerky sticks?" asked Nando.

"Yeah, yeah. I'll get 'em to you. I also got a few cans of chicken noodle soup."

Seeing that I was accommodating, Pierce upped the ante. "What about that lasagna, man? I don't want none of them soups."

"I got other people to feed, Pierce."

"You hear that?" Pierce asked Nando.

"Long as I get my jerky sticks, the guy's okay."

Pierce stared at me like the little psychopath he actually is. If I gave him that lasagna, it would leave me only three packages of the stuff for thirty days. Since I cut back on eating the prison food and am allowed a limited amount of outside food a month, that lasagna is taking on greater importance. The chicken soup has the sodium content of the Dead Sea, enough maybe to put Pierce into the hospital.

Just then, a very loud argument began on the basketball court. It sounded serious. Pierce ran off to see the action. Nando smiled, patted me on the shoulder and ambled off in the same direction. From where I was, I saw someone throw a sucker punch and a guy fall down. The guy, screaming at his attacker in Spanish, got to his feet. The argument intensified. More punches were thrown. I joined inmates from the other areas and gathered around the court. Even the zombies and the Bible group walked over to watch the slugfest. Two of the guards, billy clubs unsheathed, trotted over to the court while the other guard pulled out a walkie-talkie. Without even bothering to sort out the argument, one of the guards smashed the Hispanic guy on the side of his head. He pitched forward on to the ground, his body twitching. Blood began to drip from his ear. He groaned. The whole crowd quieted down, just as the guards intended.

A large cluster of guards came out through the revolving gate, all with billy clubs at the ready. The crowd turned and walked away in all directions. Near the weight bench, a buff black guy, skin shining with sweat, was lying on his face. I couldn't figure out what he was doing there with his face to the ground, moving around as if he were break-dancing with the dirt. As I approached, I could see a plastic shank sticking out of his back and a line of thick purple blood beginning to color the dust. Somebody's bright hope, somebody's son, was writhing, gulping and gasping. Someone yelled for the guards. This time, I turned and walked away.

I had seen maiming and killing before. The argument on the basketball court was nothing but a diversion for the real business of the yard. I never know why these things happen; maybe somebody owes money or has disrespected somebody. Nobody tells me and I don't want to know, and I may be next if I don't share that lasagna. But as I walked back toward the prison, I realized that the killing would bring about a long lockdown. I could eat the food Ed sent without being harassed by the extortionists.

O

Williams tells me that Fiedler is here for another visit. He comes; he goes. He has the luxury of knowing that I'll always be home. Even if he is being paid by the hour, I give him credit for making it up here at all. When I called him last week, he told me that he had something special to show me. When I pressed him, he said, "We think there might be some DNA in your case," not exactly words to hang my hat on. But for every wrongly convicted prisoner, the magic letters of genetics allow at least a glimpse of the Promised Land.

The weeks after the murder in the yard have been somber. Every movement, everything, is completely controlled right now. I can't understand why they make so much out of a killing. It must be the public embarrassment of losing control. For sure, it has nothing to do with sympathy for the victim.

I stand with Williams inside the room with the sliding doors. He's relentless.

"You wastin' your time with this Fiedler, man. He's got that phony Irish flatfoot with him. I got links to lawyers and investigators all over the state. Guys who could spring you from the bottom of a well."

"Not interested."

"Shit, man. You ain't going nowhere with that lawyer. He's gonna bleed you dry."

"And yours works for free, I suppose."

"Get what you pay for."

The doors don't open. God, would I hate to get stuck in here! The guard in the glass booth makes us wait deliberately. He wants to show us who the boss is.

"They've got DNA evidence." I'm not sure about the DNA evidence but I try to make Williams think I am.

"DNA? DNA? No kiddin'?"

Finally, the door slides open. As we get out, I look back and smile knowingly at Williams.

He whispers to me. "D fucking NA. Wow! On your way to the free world, my man. But don't forget: many men slip between the cup and the lip."

Fiedler and O'Keefe stand up to greet me. No Ed. Nevertheless, I'm thinking that this may be the first good moment I've had here in a long time. No, it may be the first good moment I've had since being in this place. As we sit down together, part of me doesn't want to hear what they have to say. Hope is the appetizer, disappointment the dessert. Maybe better to skip the meal altogether.

Fiedler begins. He can't hide his enthusiasm. "Joel, we got good news. Finally, good news! During the original investigation, the police found a poobic hair in your bed. A poobic hair—it may be probative." These legal words always give me hope, but they never seem to work in my favor. Maybe this time, though, maybe this time they will, whatever the fuck he means by 'probative'.

"How did you find this out, Fiedler?"

"Didn't I tell you?" Fiedler's smile is infectious. "You got the best in the business on your side." O'Keefe can't suppress a smile either. "D.D. here goes through boxes of evidence and finds a plastic prescription container—looks like nothing inside. So what does D.D. do? He opens it up."

"First, I held it up to the light, Syd."

"Yeah, to the light. He looks closely, Joel. That's what O'Keefe does. He looks closely. That's why he's the best. That's why he's the number one sleuth in America. And what do you think he sees inside the container?"

"A pubic hair. You just told me." Does my crack lawyer think I'm stupid?

"Right, Joel. A poobic hair. Now why would somebody leave a poobic hair in the evidence box?"

"Tell me. Tell me, for chrissake."

"Tell him, D.D."

O'Keefe leans in and looks around to see if anybody's listening. He speaks conspiratorially. "I looked at the ledger and it said that the hair was found in the bed. They sent it out for testing. But there's no evidence of any test being done."

Fiedler jumps in. "So what do you think we do, Joel?"

O'Keefe resumes. "We're going to test it again."

"Why don't you think it's Marsha's pubic hair? Or mine?"

"There's a good reason why the test results are not on file. The evidence gets suppressed if it makes the police look bad, especially if there's been a confession."

Why doesn't this fact surprise me? O'Keefe must have done this himself on more than a few occasions. Still, I'm encouraged. "So when can they do the test?"

O'Keefe leans back. "They? That's just it, Joel. If we wait for the state, it may take a year, even more. If we pay for it ourselves, we can get it done in a week, maybe two."

"You mean if *I* pay? Right?"

"Right, right," says Fiedler. "What's money when your freedom is at stake?"

"And how much is my freedom going to cost?"

"You don't want to pay? Wait a year instead. It's your life. But you may not have D.D. on your side anymore. Pah!"

"I only asked you how much it costs?"

"A couple o' K, give or take a K," says O'Keefe.

"Give or take? How much am I giving, because I sure won't be taking?"

"Very ironic man your client is, Fiedler."

"I'm the goose that laid the golden egg." Damned if that's not exactly what I am.

"It hasn't been easy for him, D.D. He's been through a lot." Then he says to me, "Joel, DNA is the Holy Grail of innocence work. That poobic hair may be your Holy Grail." Since when does Fiedler know about Holy Grails? "Tell him how it works, D.D."

"It's simple, Joel. We take the pubic hair to the DNA lab. Then we—"

"I'm sure you just happen to know of one, right?"

"Joel," pipes Fiedler.

"Very ironic. Very ironic. Yes, I do. Of course I do. I'm a dick. Look, who found that fucking pubic hair? Me!"

"Yes, you did. And don't think I'm not thankful."

"I'm glad you are. You fucking well should be thankful. I'm saving your ass." To Fiedler he says, "What's with this guy?"

"Okay, okay. Sorry." I have to stop dwelling on the money. If they can spring me out of here, I can always go back to cab driving and online poker. "Really, D.D., I am sorry."

"All right. So this is what we do. We take it to the lab. They run it against the state's databank. If we come up with a rapist or a felon of any sort, and anyone in the databank has to be a felon, we have our man. The case is solved. You walk out of here free." Yes, it makes sense. Suddenly the law makes sense. The law is now on my side. Two minutes ago, I was filled with suspicion; now I am flying. Now I choose to believe.

"We may not even need MacSweeney anymore," says Fiedler.

"We still need everything we can get," says O'Keefe. "A button, a shoelace, a pimp, a liar. Anything to get back to court."

Court? Did he say court? "I thought you said I walk out of here free?"

"After a trial, he meant. A new trial."

No! How much time will that take? How much more will it cost? Now I want to sink beneath the floorboards. God, do I hate the fucking law!

"What's the matter, Joel?" asks Fiedler.

"Nothing. Nothing's the matter."

"A trial may not be necessary at all," says Fiedler sympathetically. "Not at all. The judge can look at all the evidence and set you free."

"First the evidence has to be gathered," says O'Keefe.

"And the state has to do its preparation, Joel. The law is orderly."

While the law works its wonders, my life will trickle away. I have to stop thinking about it. I need patience. Taking a deep breath helps me regain my equilibrium. I stand up. At least I have the power to end the session. I shake hands with Fiedler and O'Keefe. Patience. I need patience.

O'Keefe tries to reassure me. "Hang in there, Joel." He and Fiedler head out while Williams walks over as usual.

"You got DNA?" he asks.

I nod.

"You goin' right out that slidin' door." Maybe I am. Maybe I am. "And I'll be right at your side, my brother. Whoooeee, D fuckin' NA!"

O

I am looking forward again. The truth may have been suppressed but the truth is still there. *The truth will out.* Looking forward is hope, *the thing with feathers,* as my poet calls it, and now I have it. I realize, too, that I never gave up hope. If the system really wants justice to be served, justice served instead of endless time, then I can look forward. The real murderer will be found. *Enjoy your life without,* I'll tell the real murderer, *I've warmed up your sentence for you.* I'll never be able to forget what happened, I will never get over Marsha's murder and my imprisonment, but I can live in such a way as to make up for what I failed to do the last time I was free.

All of this promise rests upon a pubic hair, a single denizen of a nest of wiry little things, normally of no significance beyond signaling the onset of puberty, so unimportant that some men now, like women, shave it off for dubious purposes. Hope must always be tempered. I keep thinking of what Fiedler told me about why the system fears wrongful convictions. All of them, Alpha/Brookes, Judge Poliakoff, Captain Swain and everyone else involved in my conviction—even the appeal judge—everyone who participated in this dance will be found wanting in some way when I walk free. All of them will face shunning; their careers will be stained. Alpha/Brookes will not become a district attorney, *the* district attorney; Judge Poliakoff will not move up to the appeal court; Captain Swain will never become a chief of police.

Marsha's family will come on TV and break down again. They will have lost their closure. They will not want to go through another trial. They will hate me even more. That feeling of relief that passed through the courtroom, that reprieve from ambiguity, will become its opposite again: anxiety and dread. How do a pubic hair, a rat-faced lawyer and an Irish flatfoot stand up against that dread? New York wants me to be guilty. New York needs me to be guilty. The taxpayers will be out millions of dollars. Even if I get out, the media will convince the public, as if it needed convincing, that I am escaping by some loophole. The politicians will look to close the loopholes even further. The wrongly convicted man who comes after me won't even be able to test a pubic hair. What is hope against these forces of ambition and retribution? How can the thing with feathers stay aloft?

○

Late that afternoon, I reach Ed at home. I want to share the hope.

"You're too high, Joel. Way too high. You're setting yourself up for a big disappointment."

Of course, when it comes to the law, I know he's right, but Ed has always believed in the evil eye. I think it's one of the reasons he has an eating disorder. If he were a bit heavier than normal, maybe more than a bit, he'd be showing off to the gods. According to Ed, even the appearance of happiness is a challenge to the gods. He thinks that if he looks as poor and miserable as possible, they won't notice him.

"I have nothing but hope to keep me going, Ed. Nothing, that's for sure. So don't tell me not to hope."

"I'm not telling you anything of the sort. Just keep it in perspective, brother. If you get too high now, you'll be lower than low if it doesn't come through for you."

"You can't think like that in here, Ed. Every day you're in here is the worst day of your life. I can't get any more depressed than I am every day, so let me get high on hope."

"Not dope? Hope, not dope!"

"I could use some of that too, Ed."

"Are they listening in?"

"Probably. Look, Ed, one of the reasons I'm calling is to ask you to come up here for a visit."

"Sure. Sure, I'll come."

"When?"

"Any time. Not this week—I've got something on—but maybe next week."

"For fuck's sake, Ed, give me a date you'll come up here. I need to see a familiar face that isn't mixed up with the law."

"I tell you, Joel, it's a long trip."

"So? What do you have to do so much?" He's pissing me off.

"All right. I'll try. Maybe next Sunday."

"Count!" booms the loudspeaker.

"You'll drive up next Sunday?"

"How am I going to drive up? You think I can afford to rent a car?"

What is my brother talking about? "Fiedler says you have a new car."

"That's what he said? That's what Fiedler said?"

"That's what he said. Yes."

"I wanted it to be a surprise, Joel." I want to rip the phone out of the wall. My brother lying unexpectedly is torture almost as great as the grind of prison.

"Count!"

"You mean you thought I would come out to the parking lot to take a look at your new car? Excuse me, at *my* new car? That we'd take a spin around the fucking neighborhood?"

"Calm down. The Porsche is yours, Joel. As soon as you get out of there, the keys are in your hand. You slide right under the steering wheel and drive us back down. I can't wait. Brother, it handles so well you'll cum in your pants!"

"That sounds just terrific."

"Joel, what's happened to you?"

"Three plus years of prison. That's what's happened. For something I didn't do. That's what's happened! Or didn't you know?"

"All right. All right. Calm down, will you?"

"You'll come up. Right?"

"I'll make every attempt."

"Good. Now listen, you're going to get a call from D.D. O'Keefe."

"The dick, yes."

"D.D. the dick." We share a laugh, our first laugh together in three years and it's not even funny. "Yeah, he needs money to pay for a DNA test."

"I thought the police do that."

"The state can take over a year. O'Keefe can get it done in two weeks."

"Sounds like this D.D. O'Keefe is a con man."

"Ed, just give him the money."

"Count!"

"How much is he asking for?"

"It'll be in the thousands, two maybe three. Look, I gotta go or I'll be cited."

"I hate to tell you this, Joel, but the well is running dry."

"What?"

"Detectives, food, legal fees. It adds up."

"I had a quarter of a million dollars in that account, Ed. A quarter of a million dollars. How much is left, brother?"

"Give or take…" He ends it there, a loose end that he won't pick up.

"Excuse me?"

"A quarter of a million dollars these days is *bubkes*. We got billionaires running around this country paying more than that for a hotel weekend."

"Count!"

"Shut the fuck up, Ed! Give O'Keefe the money! Even if you have to sell my car!"

"He'll get the money. He'll get the money. Don't worry."

"Ed, I'm drowning."

"Okay, okay. He'll be paid. Take my word for it."

"Thanks. You'll come up here?"

"Maybe. Sure. Word of honor."

O

I'm back in the hotel corridor, but the numbers are gone. I'm trudging along the low pile carpet without a signpost of any sort. What floor am I on? Where are the stairs? Where is my guide, my faded lawyer? I see a bank of elevators and press the call button. No indicator light goes on; I hear no machinery clanking. Fear possesses me; never have I felt a scintilla of such fear. I set out in the same direction. I need to find the lobby and the revolving door to the outside or else I'm done.

I wake to a smell, an infernal stink that now permeates the cell at all times. Rot. Is it me who's dying or Hernandez or both of us? The smell reminds me of my grandparents' apartment before grandma died, the smell of death before death. Hernandez is snoring, coming awake for seconds at a time, and going back to sleep. He is taking his meds and spends whatever waking hours he has in the yard with the zombies.

The lockdown has ended; the weather is finally cooling off. I got no answers today when I called Fiedler and O'Keefe. No answers yesterday or the day before either. They're probably filtering my calls. Maybe they're sharing my money at a resort in Palm Beach, toasting me with pina coladas at the poolside, "To Joel!" A good time had on me.

The newspaper in the library says that Marty Tankleff, now 34 years old, has been released from prison after seventeen years through the work of his private investigator. The prosecutors still insist that Tankleff is guilty; they just don't have the evidence to keep him incarcerated any longer. That's what they say. The state has committed two major felonies: kidnapping and forcible confinement, the very crimes it has committed against me. But those perps will serve no time for their crime. Tankleff is to blame, they say, for confessing like I did, for saying that he may have blacked out and murdered his parents for their money, his parents who loved him beyond anything else in their world. *Tankleff was the author of his own misfortune*, not a teenager falsely confessing after forty-eight straight hours of interrogation. Released without apology but released nonetheless. Some cause for hope anyway.

I don't need their apologies; I just want to see their pain. Judge Poliakoff and Alpha/Brookes and Swain cast into some ring in hell, some vision of Hieronymus Bosch turned real, stripped, whipped and sodomized by demons. That's what they deserve for taking away my life.

But, really, why blame them; they were doing what they're paid to do. Fiedler, on the other hand, could not do what he was paid to do.

"My client has been accused of murdering his wife, the woman he loved, married and lived with for five years. Why would he do such a thing? My colleague here, Mr. Brookes, the prosecutor, says that the defendant wanted her dead to avoid the consequences of fatherhood. Why wouldn't he just walk away? Nobody needs to kill their wife to escape a marriage. And where's the proof he killed her? What evidence does the state show you? He has Marsha's blood on his hands and shirt. His fingerprints are on the knife. He lives in that apartment, so why wouldn't his fingerprints be on the knife? He cut up fruit that morning. A girl sees him leaving the apartment when he said he was stuck on the subway. That Glenda, she lied to you. Obviously she lied. And then, and then...Where is it?" At that moment, Fiedler's papers went flying out of the legal file. "I got so many papers here. Wait a minute." From the floor, he said, "Here, here's what I'm getting at. Joel Ascher has a marvelous record as a cab driver in the great city of New York." Fiedler stood up and continued to ad lib. "Just like my colleague, Mr. Brookes, has a great record, unblemished. And Her Honor, Judge Poliakoff, praised for her work from the bench throughout the profession. And the police captain, have you ever seen a better investigator?" Fielder bent down, picked up and replaced the scattered papers on the defense table. No one, not even Fiedler, could have misread the silence that fell over that courtroom. Undaunted, he approached the jury and continued, "If you're going to imprison my client for the rest of his life, you better not do it with flimsy evidence like this. I've known Joel Ascher now for almost a year and he's the sweetest of guys. He never lost his temper with me, not once. The only thing this man cut up that morning or that afternoon, for that matter, was his fruit. He is incapable of cutting any other thing, maybe bread or meat or fish, but not another person, especially his beautiful wife. Please consider the evidence carefully before you do something you may regret." The jury listened with their heads bowed.

O

I've stopped making phone calls and settled back into a numb but stable state of hopeless resignation. I no longer keep track of the days. Williams' face appears at the cell door.

"Where's my man? Where's my Ascher man? I been lookin' through the institution and can't find my man." Looking at Hernandez asleep as usual, he says, "Why you staying in here with that guy? That there is a corpse. You letting yourself go again. You should be getting out in the yard. Air out there is good today. Get used to it before you leave."

Before I leave? What does he mean?

"Smells in here like the dead walkin'. Hell, smells like the devil's cabana. Maybe you want some Prozac?"

"You're out of luck for the moment, Williams."

"Your credit's always good, my man."

"Thanks."

Williams breaks into a wide grin. "You...got...visitors. Usual suspects and another guy too. Who knows, man? They might have the DNA with 'em. Who knows? D fuckin' NA. They might have your ticket's what they might have. Your ticket out."

The thing with feathers has again swooped down into the cell. I get out of bed and stand shakily. Hernandez is unconscious and it appears as if he will remain so long after my return. I, on the other hand, am suddenly awake. I was sure they had abandoned me.

Once again, I walk with Williams through the sliding doors into the cafeteria. Fiedler, his briefcase up on the table, O'Keefe and, as Williams said, another guy are sitting there waiting. They all look my way. The new guy has a dark goatee and dark-rimmed glasses; he smiles at me. Fiedler and O'Keefe appear to be deferring to him, no doubt some scientist, the DNA expert. Williams stands a little bit to the side, trying to eavesdrop. The DNA expert stares at Williams, who backs off and goes to his usual corner of the room.

"Nosy guy," says the DNA scientist whose voice sounds a little familiar. In fact he suddenly seems altogether familiar. Fiedler and O'Keefe stare at me. What the hell is going on here? "Joel," the guy says and I realize that he's not the DNA expert; he's Ed, emaciated Ed, except now he looks like a normal well-fed person with a goatee and dark rimmed glasses and a smile on his face. It's a new Ed, a fleshed out Ed. Finally!

"Jesus, Ed, you look great!"

"And you've lost weight, Joel. It kind of looks good on you too. Maybe you could use a little more sunshine."

He stands up and hugs me. I go along but I feel strange seeing him after three plus years during which he hasn't visited me a single time. I feel strange having him hug me with no explanation for his absence. I want to hear him say that he's fucked up or ask my forgiveness. How can he pretend as if he'd just gone out to the corner store and come back with the paper and a carton of milk? But I also feel good seeing him. I think that good news has come in with him, with Fiedler and O'Keefe and Ed all smiling. Maybe Ed has just been waiting for good news, just like me. Ed sits back down and I follow suit.

The four of us sit and stare at each other. I wait for someone to break the silence. Williams is looking over to us. You can see puzzlement in his body language and in the way he squinches up his face.

"All right," I say. "What gives?"

"Tell him, D.D," says Fiedler. "Joel, D.D. has news." Williams inches closer to our table, stopping when we look over to him, and continuing to come forward when we look at each other.

"The DNA test is in, Joel."

"Yes?" Maybe I'm wrong? Maybe the news is bad? Maybe Ed has come to keep me from ending my life.

"Tell him, D.D.," says Ed.

"It's not you, Joel."

"Is it Marsha?" I feel like I'm opening a report card.

"It's not Marsha."

Two steps, no bad news yet. "Who then?"

"Someone else."

"Someone in the databank?"

D.D. shakes his head. "No."

I smack the table.

"But it may be evidence that someone else was in the room." I'm not altogether comfortable with the idea that a pubic hair from someone who wasn't a criminal wound up on our sheet, although I have to admit that her infidelity would be less a mystery than her staying married to me for half a decade.

Fiedler says, "It might get us back into court."

Might? Might? Why is everything might and maybe? Goddammit, I'd like to hear something definite for once.

Fiedler continues. "We have to hear what the appeal judge has to say. We submit a 440 motion and see if the judge will give us a hearing based on new evidence. Of course Brookes will reply to our 440 asking the judge to deny us."

"How long will this take?"

"No more than a year," says Fiedler.

"A year. I have to wait a year to see if a pubic hair is…is…"

"Probative."

"And then I have to wait a year to go through a trial? Why don't all of you just sit around a table and decide? It might take ten minutes."

"I told you that you don't rush the law, Joel. I have to prepare our documents. Brookes has to prepare his response. The appeal judge has to come to a decision. He's got cases galore on his docket." Fiedler stops talking but I can see he has more to say. What isn't he telling me?

"Keep going." An ominous feeling takes hold of me.

Fiedler takes a breath. "Before you get a new trial, you have to expect that they might appeal the appeal court ruling. They have unlimited funds."

"And that's another year, right?"

O'Keefe interrupts before Fiedler can respond. "Meantime, I can continue to look for new evidence and witnesses to make your case even stronger. More than just the one affidavit you have so far."

"A poobic hair is good," says Fiedler, "but it's not powerful, unless it happens to belong to a criminal."

"Not powerful," says O'Keefe, "not powerful at all."

"What you really mean is that it's no good."

"I said that it's good, just not powerful. Brookes will call it a 'stray'." I stare at O'Keefe in bafflement. "It's something that may have been brought into the house on your clothing—or Marsha's."

"Jesus! You mean that people are walking around shedding pubic hairs in the taxis and streets of New York? And one of these stray pubic hairs happens to wind up in my bed?"

"It's probably not a stray," says O'Keefe. "Probably there's a very good reason that the pubic hair is in your bed."

Ed, who has been looking on quietly, speaks reassuringly. "Joel, you have to be patient. We're all in this thing together."

"How can I go on for another three years? Three years! And you said the well is running dry."

Fiedler and O'Keefe exchange glances. Fielder says, "Maybe they won't appeal. Of course you could also lose. Who knows?" Ed turns in my direction and gestures for them to move away.

"Gotta get back to work, Joel," says O'Keefe, getting to his feet. Fiedler follows suit and they both walk toward the exit. Williams starts to come over but stops when he sees that Ed remains behind.

"You shouldn't broadcast it, Joel. I was just cautioning you. I can see it coming down the pipe but we haven't gotten there just yet."

"Are you still collecting rent on the apartment?"

"Um, no. You see, Joel, I've kind of moved in there for now."

"You left home and now you're paying the maintenance on my apartment? That's why the well is running dry, isn't it? Because, Ed, I know you don't have a pot to piss in."

"I got a part-time job as a computer programmer."

"You work part time and you can pay maintenance on the Upper East Side?"

"Actually, Joel, I'm not living there by myself." What next? "I'm cohabiting...with a really great woman. A professional. I'm going to bring Bianca up here so the two of you can meet. She knows that you're wrongly convicted. You'll really like her, Joel. She's a very sweet person."

Why is my voice caught back in my throat? I should be happy. I've been able to help my brother turn his life around.

"She has a great job and pulls in a good salary." Why am I not feeling any joy for him? "I want you to know that we've kept the furniture the same, the kitchen appliances, everything except the bed. The bed...you know."

"Thanks, Ed."

"Having your brother in the apartment is a helluva lot better than letting renters ruin the place. Bianca and I take really good care of it."

Why do I want to punch my brother in the face?

Ed pulls out a sheaf of papers and a fancy pen from his jacket pocket. "Look, Joel, I've brought along some papers here. I need you to sign in three places. It's a transfer of ownership, mainly for insurance purposes. They won't continue to insure a property when the owner is no longer on the premises and, of course, you're not on the premises. This way..." he stops. "Don't look at me that way. We can't insure the place without the owner on the premises. What if there's a fire?" Another one of Hamlet's lines, or is it Macbeth or whoever and I don't give a damn, comes to me: *My gorge rises.* That's what is stuck in my throat. My gorge.

"Put it on the market. Sell it."

Ed chuckles. "Christ, Joel."

"Sell it, Ed, and put the money in my account."

"No fucking way I'm going to sell it. The market stinks right now."

"I want you to sell it!"

"Relax. Let's wait a year and see how things stack up. You may even want to move back in when you get out of here. Just sign the papers. For now."

"I said 'sell it'!"

"Calm down, Joel. This is no time to make a decision like that."

"Sell it!"

"You always were a powder keg."

I stand up and pull my brother off his chair by the lapels of his sport jacket. Yanking his face into mine, I shake him back and forth like a rag doll. The buttons are popping off his shirt while his eyes are popping out of his head.

"Ascher, man, get your hands off him!" Williams starts over to where we're standing.

I pull Ed down to the floor and start pounding his face with my fists. He covers up. Williams pulls me off him, tossing me aside into a cafeteria table. I am gored.

The soon-to-be-pensioned guard stashes his porn magazine and pulls out his walkie-talkie. He comes over to where my brother is hyperventilating. "You okay?"

I hear a voice on the other end of the walkie-talkie: "Yeah?"

"Get a couple of guys down here to the caf. We got an incident."

Ed's nose is dripping blood that he wipes with the sleeve of his sport jacket. Williams reaches out and asks if he's okay. He pushes Williams' hand away. "Don't worry about me, bud." The pain in my thigh where my leg hit the table is acute. Ed stares at me and speaks with the kind of hate that can only be expressed by people who have grown up in the same family. "Who gave you the idea that you have any rights at all, brother? You're a nothing. No, you're worse than nothing. You're below zero, a wife killer. A sick fuck! I hope with all my heart that you never see the outside of this place again. Better yet, save the state some money and die." My brother, his blood dripping a trail on to the floor that I had polished, starts to walk off but is held back by the desk guard.

"Hang in, we'll need to file a report."

O

You assaulted your own brother. No reason, really. But you got one thing out of it, didn't you, Ascher? You got a sentence for a determined time and an understandable reason, a sixty days sentence within a life sentence within the sentence that is now my life, like a set of Russian dolls. Even if Ed presses charges, they can't add to your sentence.

And you didn't mind much being here all this time, did you, Ascher? You were sealed off from the noise and stink and society of the prison. Of course you had to talk to yourself to the point of insanity and listen to your heartbeat like a character out of Edgar Allan Poe. And you were stared at in your five by seven cell by the red light of a camera. If you started banging your head against the wall, they would have come running. What was the best part? The silent guards delivering a food tray or accompanying you to one hour of exercise every other day or maybe your twice-weekly shower? The prison letting you have conjugal visits with a poetry book? If it weren't for Emily, you'd have gone past that point of insanity. You found some of her poems harder to understand than the Sunday

Times crossword but so what? She was there for you.
> *Erase the root—no tree—*
> *Thee—then—no me—*
    Emily had lived alone too, a perfect cellmate. You gave her more attention than you did your wife.

    Remember when you first saw Marsha seated on the curb outside Bloomingdale's, having just broken her high heel and fallen over, bruising her knee and twisting her ankle. Solicitous people were standing around as they always do for good-looking people. You jumped out of the cab and helped her inside, driving her down to Cabrini Hospital. You stayed with her for hours in the waiting room, soothing her pain, and remained there until she got an examination, a pain killer prescription and an ankle brace. You picked up the Oxycontin, took her home, and struck up a conversation. You, Ascher! This incredibly beautiful woman was talking to you and you kept wondering, 'How can I keep this going'?

    You got her phone number—a miracle, you thought. You were so afraid of losing the number that you wrote it down on four other pieces of paper. You let her into your life, she met Mel and Debra, and, after six months, you got married. She agreed to a small wedding since you have no friends and you didn't want the parties too unbalanced. And then, before too long, you tried to disappear. You resented her getting in the way of what you wanted to do. You argued about that for five years. Then an amnesty was declared. You began making love again, agreed she didn't have to use protection. The fear took hold of you, the fear of losing your otherwise pointless existence. You had everything you wanted and two things you didn't want: a woman who loved you and, just around the corner, a little baby to love. Face the truth, Ascher. You've lived in solitary for almost forty years.

> *The Soul unto itself*
> *Is an imperial friend—*
> *Or the most agonizing Spy*
> *An Enemy—could send—*

Some bastard killed her but you would have done it in your own way. For that crime you had yet to commit, you are living in prison for the remainder of your natural life.

Williams. "Get your ass up, my man. They letting you have a legal visit."

When did I see him last? "Yeah? Who?" My voice sounds so unfamiliar to me that I can only speak in monosyllables.

"Who do you think, man?"

Surely not.

"Sure you don't want one of my guys?" I can't even bother answering. Williams ushers me to the cafeteria where Fiedler, yes, my lawyer of record, sits alone. What is he doing here? He stands up as I walk over. The desk guard puts his porn aside and Williams stands closer than usual. Fiedler hugs me while I stand there stiffly.

"Joel, Joel, Joel, you look terrible." I just nod. He motions kindly with his hand. "Sit down, Joel. Sit down." We take our seats at the table. "You want something from the machines?"

I keep nodding. Fiedler brings back two fish sandwiches with a Diet Pepsi. I would probably have chosen the fish myself.

"I can't pay."

"On the house."

I shake my head.

"I know, I know, you can't pay me. Some brother."

Fiedler waits while I wolf down the two sandwiches.

"Where do we go from here, Joel?"

I point in the general direction of the rear of the prison. "There's a cemetery."

"You don't give up. You have to keep trying." I stare at him, thinking that he's failed to get the message.

"It's over. I can't pay for anything."

"No, it's not. It's never over if you want to prove your innocence."

I wave my hand at him. "Why don't you leave me alone?"

"I like you, Joel. I see you like a son. The son I never had."

The son he never had. That makes two of us. "You couldn't have children?"

"I couldn't have a wife."

"Too busy, huh, Syd?"

"Yeah, I'm too busy. I'm always busy. A rolling stone."

"You weren't in Yonkers that day, were you?"

My comment is mistimed of course; I had mulled over my interrogation during my time in solitary. Fiedler stares at me while recalling the day himself. He shakes his head. "I'm sorry, Joel. It wasn't good."

It wasn't good.

"They give my name to suspects who don't have lawyers."

"Because you're the worst lawyer in New York City, right?"

"Your case would have been tough even for Johnnie Cochran, may he rest in peace. The blood was a big problem. And what am I going to do with the pictures he shows and the confession that he keeps playing over and over? And where were the witnesses to back up your alibi? Is it my fault that nobody notices you except that girl, someone who didn't even see you? 'What kind of cockamamie case is this'? I ask myself."

"Maybe you're right."

"I didn't know what to believe, Joel."

What's the matter with me? I feel sorry for this man. He fucked up the summation, complimented everyone who was trying to put me in prison and cost me the rest of my life. Yet I feel sorry for him. I am not a real man; I'm pathetic, *a nothing*, as Ed said, a cipher.

"So where do we go from here, Joel?"

"How about MacSweeney? We haven't tried him yet."

"MacSweeney." Fiedler smiles. "Now you're talking."

"Fiedler, you're a good man. A nice man." I reach out and put my hand on his arm. "But I can't accept your services anymore."

He looks at me uncomprehendingly. "You expect to get yourself out of prison?" His arm is thin; like the rest of him, a sure candidate for osteoporosis.

He looks up. "You don't trust me?"

"Sure I trust you, Fiedler. I just don't trust the law."

"The more reason you need a lawyer. I'll work for nothing."

"Is that right?" I'm touched. He's offering to be a lifeline. What would be the point of refusing? Maybe a bad lawyer is better than none. "Okay, Syd. I'll call you if I get any bright ideas."

"I'll be here in a jiffy."

"And bring MacSweeney with you."

The old man beams and then he hugs me. "Next time."

"You never know, Fiedler, MacSweeney may be the answer."

Walking me back from this meeting to my cell, my final day in solitary, Williams pulls a letter from inside his shirt. The return address, my return address, tells me it's from Ed. I rip it open. No salutation, no yours truly, no love, no signature. Just a typed note:

The apartment began to feel too small for us. We've started emptying out. Salvation Army loved your clothes; Bianca fits right into Marsha's. Left your LPs at the curb.

O

Halloween. I went to spend some time out on the yard today and dragged Hernandez with me for protection, although I wasn't certain that a drugged up psycho could afford me much protection. We were pale enough to pass as ghosts. Sure enough, Pierce and Nando, the two hyenas, set their sights on me. I hadn't been outside for over two months and you could see that they were on the hunt for chocolate chip cookies, lasagna and jerky sticks. When they recognized Hernandez, they became friendly.

"Hey, bro, what you got for me today? I mean like trick or treat."

"Sorry, Pierce, but I've been cut off."

"No shit?"

"Yeah, I'm sorry. I still have some chicken soup left over if you want it."

"*Que pasa?*" Nando asked Hernandez. I think it was the only question that Hernandez could have answered.

"*Nada.*"

"Come on, Nando, the guy's a useless asshole." I assumed Pierce was referring to me. They walked off together; Pierce didn't seem to have given the chicken soup the slightest consideration. He was a lot smarter than I had given him credit for.

I sat down in the dust and Hernandez sat alongside me. It was a cool gray day but I found it a relief just to be outside. I put my arm around Hernandez' shoulders; I didn't give a shit what the others thought. I could follow his example and seek oblivion, asking the so-called prison doctor in the so-called infirmary for anti-psychotic medication so I could join the growing klatch of zombies circling the yard. All I need to do is start behaving strangely, pretend I'm hearing voices or having hallucinations, and he'd provide me with a lifetime prescription, one pill per morning till I die, dispensed by the so-called nurse. As a bonus, I would damage my liver, shortening my life expectancy.

I noticed Kirby, another of the wrongly convicted, doing his usual run in a sweat suit around the perimeter. He stays in shape, physically and mentally, so he can continue to fight for his innocence and eventual release. He copped a plea, fifteen years to life like I was offered, so the judges don't even read his self-made motions. If I decide to take more years trying to overturn my conviction, I will go on a letter writing campaign to enlist the services of an innocence project. Fat chance. There are fifty innocence projects in America and thirty thousand wrongly convicted prisoners vying for attention. But then I'm luckier than most; I have Fiedler. I'll spend the whole day like Kirby, thinking about my case, and hope one day the big breakthrough will come. Maybe O'Keefe, from the goodness of his heart, will work for me again. He will uncover a note, an e-mail, from...from Carlos the doorman to Marsha, telling her how much he loved her and how much he hated me. They will discover her reply e-mail rejecting his advances. Carlos will cave in to police interrogation, admit to having let himself into the apartment with the master key and, in a fit of jealous rage, committing the murder. A judge's order will set me free. Television cameras will record the moment when I, flanked by my team of lawyers, all right, with Syd Fiedler and D.D. O'Keefe, walk out the prison gate. In an interview in front of cameras and a bank of microphones, I'll be conciliatory, saying how our justice system in America, for all of its flaws, eventually gets it right. I'll forgive everyone involved in my wrongful conviction. "I'm not bitter. I'm not angry. I just want to start over and put the lost years behind me." And all the while I'll be thinking how we'll sue their asses. We'll sue their asses, imagining old Pearlstone packing up his stethoscope and tongue depressors, contemplating his ruined reputation; the fucking barber pole's photo in the newspaper with a story about the dozen false confessions he's manufactured; the grease head facing a disciplinary board for malicious prosecution; the judge thrown off the bench, her puffed head rolling out the courtroom door. I'll sue their asses! But then—it's our legal system, after all—a smug, supercilious, self-satisfied state appeal judge will say that I confessed, making me, like Marty Tankleff, the author of my own misfortune and therefore ineligible for a dime of compensation. Oh, how well the fuckers will cover for each other! Don't they always. I can't even beat them in my daydreams.

Better to give up and snack on *that pale sustenance, despair*, accept the status quo, ruminate, mop and wax, kill vermin, flies and other pests and rot in my rancid cell. That lifestyle will require something besides anti-psychotics. I'll go to Williams for little blue sleeping pills to shut down my overactive brain. Williams can slip me one a day for a dollar a pop. I'd promise not to accumulate them and commit suicide; I wouldn't want him to face prosecution.

I then noticed the God and Jesus bunch walking past with their lay preacher, a big bright African American, a former football player named Woods, who had brought with him into the prison his rolling thunder of a voice and his repertoire of Biblical lore. Every day in America, less capable but equally determined Bible thumping evangelicals, former alcoholics and cat burglars, fan out across the prisons searching for lost and needy souls, like tow truck drivers searching for car wrecks. The morose old chaplain sits by himself in the prison chapel, knowing that he doesn't stand a chance against these guys. Most of the prisoners start out just wanting to talk to some halfway-intelligent person and wind up becoming born again Christians. The God and Jesus bunch always ignores me because they know I'm not a Christian in the first place. But I got up, leaving Hernandez behind with a dazed look on his face. I followed the group and the preacher to a remote corner of the yard and stuck my nose into the prayer session. For a moment, I just wanted to be around people who believe in something, who believe that things will get better some time, even if that time will be beyond time. Woods was talking about the Wandering Jew—it almost seemed deliberate—the guy who refused to help Jesus on his way to the cross and was punished for his lack of charity, punished by having to come back one day every year until Jesus' second coming. Compared to prison, that seemed like a decent fate. When Woods finished his sermon, he acknowledged my presence, while the others, one by one, took my hands in theirs and welcomed me. Now that's a future! Future shlock.

Wait a minute! What am I thinking? Aha! Maybe it *was* Carlos the doorman! He had the time; he had the opportunity. Did he have the motive? Did he have the motive? Maybe he had a close relative who wanted the apartment? Ridiculous! Maybe he *was* having an affair with Marsha? When I returned to the apartment the *day of*, Carlos wasn't wearing the topcoat of his uniform, his top hat or his white gloves. His livery. Isn't that what it's called? He wasn't in livery. I thought he removed his livery because of the heat. Idiot, he must have thrown it all out because his gloves and topcoat were smeared with Marsha's blood! The gloves, of course, the gloves! That's why only my fingerprints were on the knife!

We'll get the police to question Carlos and demand he provide a DNA sample. The DNA testers along with state officials, troubled that an innocent man might have wasted years of his life in prison, will be standing at the ready when Carlos's blood sample is delivered to the state lab. And they will test…and they will test…and they will find that Carlos Estevez's DNA matches the DNA from the pubic hair found on our bed. They will arrest him and charge him. The apologies will begin. The compensation for the lost years will be announced. I'll be back in court for a new judge to release me and…no, don't give in to the thing with feathers. Not again. But is there another suspect even possible, another explanation for what happened? There always is, but no, not this time. Carlos killed Marsha, definitely, plunged in the knife, and then stood at the front door of the building while I was taken in for questioning. He stood there secretly laughing at me, this shmuck of a husband, probably thinking that anyone who failed to love this woman, to love her like he did, deserved what he was getting.

I will call Fiedler. Yes, Fiedler will be here, as he promised, in a jiffy. And yes, I will be free! I will be free!

You, goddess of Hope, you who are left when all else has departed, are a tempter no less skilled than the Devil.